MASTER ZACHARIUS,
GIL BRALTAR,
A DRAMA IN THE AIR.

ABOUT THE AUTHOR.

Jules Verne was born in Nantes, France in 1828. In his lifetime, over fifty of his wondrous adventure stories were published by J. Hetzel & Co. in the Extraordinary Journeys series, including the world-famous *Journey to the Center of the Earth*, *Twenty Thousand Leagues Under the Seas*, and *Around the World in Eighty Days*. He died in 1905.

JULES VERNE.

MASTER ZACHARIUS,
GIL BRALTAR,
A DRAMA IN THE AIR.

TRANSLATED FROM THE FRENCH BY
GRIGORY FOZIMIR.

WITH TWENTY ILLUSTRATIONS BY
TH. SCHULER; G. ROUX; E. BAYARD AND A. MARIE.

INCLUDES A GLOSSARY OF UNCOMMON WORDS.

TEPLEV BOOKS.

TEPLEV MEDIA PTY. LTD.

MELBOURNE.

2024.

Teplev Books.
Published by Teplev Media Pty. Ltd., Melbourne, Australia.
www.teplevmedia.com

First edition published 2024.

These short stories are translations of literary works of fiction.

Original French publications: "Maître Zacharius : ou l'Horloger qui avait perdu son âme," *Musée des familles*, 1854. "Gil Braltar," *Le Petit Journal*, 1887. "Un voyage en ballon," *Musée des familles*, 1851.

Typeset in Libre Baskerville.

A catalogue record for this book is available from the National Library of Australia.

I.S.B.N.: 978-0-6483379-2-8 (paperback)

I-06.05.2024

CONTENTS.

TRANSLATOR'S NOTE.

Jules Verne had a delightfully dramatic and captivating way of styling his prose writing in French. For one thing, he used exclamation marks copiously, which adds intensity. For another thing, in his sentences he often strung multiple clauses together in long clause chains and put important actions or information in the final clauses, which adds to the suspense and helps to carry the reader's attention along on the adventure.

It would be wrong to suppress these idiosyncratic stylistic features in an English translation merely to satisfy the whims and fancies of a translator who presumed to know better than the author; particularly when such features can, for the most part, be translated perfectly well from French. Ideally, a translator should be a humble conduit for the author's work, transmitting it in its entirety from one code into another as seamlessly as he is able.

The translation objective for the three short stories in this volume was to reproduce the letter and the spirit of the original French texts as accurately and faithfully as possible in fluent English. To this end, the original paragraphs, indents, sentence structures, repetitions, punctuation, italicizations, and variant personal and place name spellings have been retained where practicable.

It is an honor and a privilege to have the good Fortune in life to be able to translate the works of such a literary genius as Jules Verne. If he could read over these translations and be satisfied that justice had been done to his works, then this translator's aim would have been achieved. May readers be enchanted by these wondrous, entertaining stories.

G. Fozimir.

Melbourne, May 2024.

MASTER ZACHARIUS.

I.

A WINTER'S NIGHT.

The city of Geneva is located at the western point of the lake to which it gave or owes its name. The River Rhone, which runs through it as it exits the lake, divides it into two distinct districts, and is itself divided, at the center of the city, by an island cast between its two banks. This topographical configuration often occurs in large centers of commerce or industry. No doubt the first indigenous people were enticed by the transport facilities which the fast-flowing arms of the rivers offered them, "these pathways that move on their own," in the words of Pascal. As for the Rhone, these are pathways that run.

In the time when new and regular constructions were not yet springing up on this island, anchored like a Dutch galliot in the middle of the river, the marvelous heap of houses climbing on top of one another offered a charming jumble to the eye. The small area of the island had forced some of these constructions to perch on piles, driven pell-mell into the harsh currents of the Rhone. These large beams, blackened with time, worn down by the waters, resembled the claws of a huge crab and produced a fantastic effect. A few yellowed nets, veritable spiderwebs hanging beneath the age-old substructure, stirred in the shadows as if they were the foliage of old oak trees, and the river, rushing into the midst of this forest of piles, foamed with a lugubrious murmur.

One of the residences on this island was striking in its strangely dilapidated character. It was the house of the old clockmaker, Master Zacharius, his daughter, Gerande, Aubert Thun, his apprentice, and his old maidservant, Scholastique.

What a man apart this Zacharius was! His age seemed indecipherable. None of the oldest people of Geneva could have said for how long his thin and pointy head had been teetering on his shoulders, nor on which day, for the first time, he had been seen walking through the streets of the city, with his long white head of hair being blown about by the four winds. This man did not live. He oscillated, like the pendulums in his clocks. His face, dry and deathly pale, affected dark hues. Like Leonardo da Vinci's paintings, he had grown darker with time.

Gerande lived in the most beautiful room in the old house, from where, by a narrow window, her view came to rest melancholily on the snowy peaks of the Jura; however, the old man's bedroom and workshop occupied a kind of cellar, situated almost at the level of the river, and whose floor rested directly on the piles. Since time immemorial, Master Zacharius only went out at mealtimes and when he went to regulate the different clocks of the city. He spent the rest of his time at a workbench covered with numerous clock-making instruments, which he had for the most part invented.

For this was a skillful man. His works were highly prized in all of France and Germany. The most industrious craftsmen in Geneva held his superiority in high esteem, and it was an honor for the people of the city, who pointed him out saying:

"To him belongs the glory of having invented the escapement!"

Indeed, from this invention, which Zacharius' works will make understood later, dates the birth of true clockmaking.

Now, after having worked long and marvelously hard, Zacharius slowly put his tools back in place, covered the fine pieces which he had just fine-tuned with light bell jars, and put the active wheel of his lathe to rest; then he lifted up the trapdoor built into the floor of his tiny room, and there, reclining for whole hours, while the Rhone rushed with a fracas before his eyes, he became intoxicated by its foggy vapors.

One winter's night, old woman Scholastique served supper, in which, according to ancient custom, she partook with the young apprentice. And even though carefully prepared foods were offered to him in beautiful blue and white crockery dishes, Master Zacharius did not eat. He hardly replied to the soft words of Gerande, who was visibly preoccupied with her father's increasingly gloomy taciturnity, and even Scholastique's babbling struck his ears no more than the rumblings of the river to which he no longer paid any attention. After this silent meal, the old clockmaker left the table without kissing his daughter, and without wishing everybody a good evening, as was customary. He disappeared through the narrow door which lead to his retreat, and, under his heavy steps, the staircase moaned with hefty groans.

Gerande, Aubert, and Scholastique remained silent for a few moments. On that evening, the weather was gloomy; the clouds

And there, reclining for whole hours... (p. 8.)

crawled heavily along the length of the Alps and threatened to bring rain; the harsh temperatures of Switzerland filled the soul with sorrow, while the south wind prowled around the surroundings and let out a sinister whistling.

"Well, are you aware, my dear young lady," said Scholastique finally, "that our master has withdrawn into himself over the last few days? Blessed Virgin! I understand why he has not been hungry, for his words have stayed in his stomach, and the devil who could draw one out of him would have to be very clever indeed!"

"My father is troubled by some secret source of grief at which I cannot even guess," replied Gerande, as a sorrowful disquiet imprinted itself upon her face.

"Young lady, do not allow such sadness to take over your heart. You know Master Zacharius' singular habits. Who could read his secret thoughts from his brow? Some trouble has no doubt beset him, but, tomorrow, he won't remember it and he will truly regret having caused any grief for his daughter."

It was Aubert who spoke in this way, fixing his gaze on Gerande's beautiful eyes. Aubert, the only apprentice whom Master Zacharius had ever taken into his confidence regarding his works, for he valued his intelligence, his discretion, and his great kindness of heart; Aubert had become attached to Gerande with that mysterious faith which presides over heroic devotion.

Gerande was eighteen years old. The oval of her face recalled those of the naive Madonnas that worshippers still put up on street corners in the old cities of Britain. Her eyes breathed an infinite simplicity. She was loved, like the sweetest creation of a poet's dream. Her clothes affected subdued colors, and the white linen which wrapped around her shoulders had that tint and that scent which were peculiar to church linens. She lived a mystical existence in this city of Geneva, which had not yet given itself over to the dryness of Calvinism.

Just as, morning and night, she read her Latin prayers from her iron-clasped missal, Gerande had read a hidden sentiment in Aubert Thun's heart, such profound devotion the young apprentice had for her. Indeed, in his eyes, the entire world was reduced to the old clockmaker's house, and all his time was spent close to the young girl, when, having finished his work, he would leave her father's workshop.

Old woman Scholastique saw this, but didn't say a word about it. Her loquacity was exercised by preference on the woes of her time and the little miseries of housekeeping. Nobody attempted to put a stop to it. She was just like one of those musical snuffboxes which are made in Geneva: once it has started up, one would have to break it to stop it from playing out all its tunes.

On finding Gerande wallowing in sorrowful silence, Scholastique left her old wooden chair, affixed a candle to the top of a candlestick, lit it, and put it down next to a small wax virgin sheltered in its stone recess. It was the custom to kneel before this Madonna, protector of the domestic hearth, asking it to extend its benevolent grace over the coming night; however, on this evening, Gerande remained silent in her place.

"Eh, well! my dear young lady," said Scholastique with surprise, "supper is finished, and now it's time to say goodnight. Do you wish to tire out your eyes with prolonged vigils?... Ah! Blessed Virgin! in any event, one must sleep and find a little bit of joy in sweet dreams! In this accursed age in which we live, who can promise a day of happiness?"

"Should we not send for a doctor for my father?" asked Gerande.

"A doctor!" exclaimed the old maidservant. "Has Master Zacharius ever lent his ear to all their fancies and opinions! There may be medicines for watches, but not for the body!"

"Then what are we to do?" murmured Gerande. "Has he resumed his work? has he given himself over to rest?"

"Gerande," replied Aubert softly, "Master Zacharius is vexed by some kind of moral affliction, and that is all."

"Do you know what it is, Aubert?"

"Perhaps, Gerande."

"Tell us what it is," exclaimed Scholastique brusquely, extinguishing her candle parsimoniously.

"For several days, Gerande," said the young apprentice, "an absolutely incomprehensible phenomenon has been occurring. All the watches that your father has made and sold in the last few years have suddenly stopped working. A great many of them have been returned to him. He carefully took them apart; the springs were in good condition and the cogs were perfectly aligned. He put them back together with even greater care; however, despite his skill, they no longer work.

"The devil is behind this!" cried Scholastique.

"What are you trying to say?" asked Gerande. "The facts of the matter appear quite natural to me. Everything on earth has its limits, and the infinite cannot be produced by the hand of man."

"It is no less true," replied Aubert, "that there is something extraordinary and mysterious in all of this. I myself assisted Master Zacharius in investigating the cause of this malfunctioning of his watches, I could not find it, and, more than once, the tools fell from my hands in despair."

"Well," continued Scholastique, "why devote oneself to all this reprobate work? Is it at all natural that a small copper instrument can work of its own accord and mark the hours? We should have stuck with the sundial!"

"You won't be talking like that any longer, Scholastique," replied Aubert, "once you learn that the sundial was invented by Cain."

"Good Lord! what are you telling me?"

"Do you really think," continued Gerande innocently, "that we could pray to God to breathe life back into my father's watches?"

"Without any doubt," replied the young apprentice.

"Well! Such prayers are useless," muttered the old maidservant, "but heaven will forgive the intention."

The candle was relit. Scholastique, Gerande, and Aubert kneeled down on the room's paving stones, and the young girl prayed for the soul of her mother, for the sanctification of the night, for travelers and prisoners, for the good and for the wicked, and, most of all, for her father's unknown sorrows.

These three devout individuals then stood up with some faith in their hearts, for they had surrendered their troubles unto the bosom of God.

Aubert returned to his room, Gerande sat very pensively by her window, as the last lights went out in the city of Geneva, and Scholastique, after having poured some water on the blazing firebrands and having slid the two enormous bolts across the door, threw herself onto her bed, where in no time she was dreaming that she was dying of fear.

And yet, the horror of this winter's night increased. From time to time, along with the whirlpools in the river, the wind howled beneath the piles, and the entire house trembled; but the young girl, absorbed in her sorrows, thought only of her father. After Aubert Thun's words, Master Zacharius' affliction had taken on fantastical proportions in her eyes, and it seemed to her that this

The young girl prayed for the soul... (p. 12.)

dear existence, having become entirely mechanical, rotated on its worn-out pivots only with great effort.

Suddenly, a window shutter, whipped violently by a gust of wind, struck the room's window. Gerande shuddered and got up abruptly, not knowing the cause of the noise which had shaken her from her stupor. As soon as her emotions had calmed, she opened the window frame. The clouds had erupted, and torrential rain splattered onto the surrounding rooves. The young girl leaned outside to catch the shutter that was being tossed about by the wind, but she was full of fear. It appeared to her that the rain and the river, combining their tumultuous waters, were engulfing the fragile house, whose boards creaked on all sides. She wanted to flee her room; but she noticed beneath her the reflection of a light which must have come from Master Zacharius' tiny room, and, during one of those calm moments when the elements go quiet, her ears were struck with plaintive sounds. She tried to shut her window but could not manage it. The wind pushed her back violently, like a criminal breaking into a house.

Gerande thought she was going mad with terror! What indeed was her father doing? She opened the door, which slipped out of her hands and banged loudly under the force of the storm. Gerande then found herself in the dark dining room, she managed, groping along, to reach the staircase which led to Master Zacharius' workshop, and, pale and faint, she let herself slip inside.

The old clockmaker was standing in the middle of the room, which was filled with the murmur of the river. His ruffled hair gave him a sinister appearance. He spoke, he gesticulated, without seeing, without hearing! Gerande stayed at the threshold.

"This is death!" said Master Zacharius in a muffled voice, "this is death!... What's left for me to live on, now that I have distributed my life force throughout the world! since I, Master Zacharius, I am the very creator of all of those watches that I have made! It is a part of my very soul that I enclosed in each of those cases of iron, silver, and gold! Every time that one of these confounded clocks stops working, I can feel my heart, which stops beating, for I tuned them to its pulse!"

And, speaking in this strange way, the old man cast his eyes over his workbench. All the parts of a watch that he had carefully taken apart were to be found there. He took a sort of hollow cylinder, called a barrel, in which the spring is enclosed, and he removed from it the steel spiral which, instead of unwinding, according to the laws of elasticity, remained coiled up, just like a sleeping viper. It appeared to be all knotted up, like one of those crippled old men whose blood eventually coagulates. Master Zacharius tried in vain to unroll it with his scrawny fingers, the silhouette of which stretched disproportionately along the wall, but he was unable to do it, and, soon, with a terrible cry of anger, he hurled it through the trapdoor into the eddies of the Rhone.

Gerande, with her feet nailed to the floor, remained without a sound, without moving. She wanted to approach her father but she couldn't. She was seized with dizzying hallucinations. Suddenly, from the shadows, she heard a voice whisper in her ear:

"Gerande, my dear Gerande! Distress is keeping you awake still! Go back to bed, I beg you, the night is cold."

"Aubert!" whispered the young girl in a low voice. "It's you! it's you!"

"Should I not concern myself with that which concerns you!" replied Aubert.

These gentle words made the blood return to the young girl's heart. She leaned on the young apprentice's arm and said to him:

"My father is quite ill, Aubert! You alone can cure him, for the ailment of his soul will not yield to the consolations of his daughter. His mind has been afflicted with an altogether natural illness, and, in working with him to repair his watches, you shall bring him back to reason. Aubert, is it not true," she added, still very affected, "that his life is fused with those of his clocks?"

Aubert did not reply.

"But would such a craft, my father's craft, not be condemned by heaven?" said Gerande, shuddering.

"I don't know," replied the apprentice, who warmed the young girl's icy hands with his. "But return to your room, my poor Gerande, and, with some rest, regain some hope!"

Gerande returned slowly to her room, and there she stayed until daybreak, without any sleep having weighed upon her eyelids, whereas Master Zacharius, staying still and silent, watched the river flow noisily beneath his feet.

II.

THE PRIDE OF SCIENCE.

The strictness of Genevan merchants with regard to business affairs has become proverbial. It is of a rigid integrity and an excessive uprightness. What must Master Zacharius' shame have been, then, when he saw those watches, which he had made with a such great care, being returned to him from all quarters.

Now, it was certain that the watches had stopped suddenly and without any apparent reason. The cogs were in good condition and were perfectly aligned, but the springs had lost all their elasticity. The clockmaker tried in vain to replace them: but the cogs remained motionless. This inexplicable malfunctioning did great harm to Master Zacharius. His magnificent inventions had repeatedly left suspicions of sorcery hanging over him, and these gained ground ever after. These rumors made their way to Gerande, and she frequently feared for her father when malicious looks were fixed on him.

However, the day after that night of anxieties, Master Zacharius appeared to resume his work with some confidence. The morning sun gave him a little courage. Aubert did not delay in joining him in his workshop and received a "good morning" full of affability.

"I'm doing better," said the old clockmaker. "I don't know what strange headaches plagued me yesterday, but the sun has chased away all of that along with the nighttime clouds."

"My goodness! master," replied Aubert, "I don't like the nighttime for you, nor for me!"

"And you are right, Aubert! If you ever become a great man, you shall understand that the daytime is as necessary for you as food! A scholar of great merit is indebted to the respects paid by the rest of mankind."

"Master, that's the sin of pride taking over you."

"Of pride, Aubert! Destroy my past, annihilate my present, squander my future, and then it would be permitted for me to live in obscurity! Poor boy who does not comprehend the sublime things with which my art is inextricably bound! Are you naught but a tool in my hands?"

"Nevertheless, Master Zacharius," continued Aubert, "I have more than once earned your praises for the way in which I fine-tuned the most delicate parts of your watches and your clocks!"

"Without any doubt, Aubert," replied Master Zacharius, "you are a good worker whom I like; but, when you work, you think that between your fingers you have naught but copper, gold, or silver, and you do not sense these metals, which my genius animates, pulsating like living flesh! Therefore, you yourself shall not die from the death of your works!"

Master Zacharius became silent after these words; but Aubert sought to continue the conversation.

"Goodness gracious me! master," he said, "I do like to see you working relentlessly like this! You'll be ready for our guild's celebration, for I can see that work on the crystal watch is progressing apace."

"Without a doubt, Aubert," exclaimed the old clockmaker, "and this shall be no small honor for me, to have been able to shape and cut this material which is as hard as diamond! Ah! Louis Berghem did well to perfect the diamond dealers' art, which has allowed me to polish and cut the hardest of stones!"

At that moment, Master Zacharius was holding some small clock parts which were made of cut crystal and were of an exquisite workmanship. The cogs, the pivots, and the casing of this watch were made of the same material, and he had, on this extremely difficult piece of work, expended unimaginable skill.

"Is it not so," he continued, as his cheeks flushed, "that it will be beautiful to see this watch beating through its transparent casing, and to be able to count the beats of its heart!"

"I wager, master," replied the young apprentice, "that it will not waver by even a second per year!"

"And you would be wagering with certainty! Have I not put the purest part of myself into it? Does my own heart waver?"

Aubert did not dare to look directly up at his master.

"Speak to me frankly," replied the old man melancholily. "Have you never taken me for a fool? Do you not think that I have occasionally indulged in disastrous follies? Yes, is it not so! In my daughter's eyes, and in yours, I have often read my condemnation.—Oh!" he cried with sorrow, "to not even be understood by the beings that one loves the most in the world! But to you, Aubert, I shall prove triumphantly that I am right! Do not shake your head, for you shall be astonished! The day when you know how to listen to me and to understand me, you shall see that I have discovered the secrets of existence, the secrets of the mysterious union between the body and the soul!"

In speaking like this, Master Zacharius showed himself to be filled with hubris. His eyes shone with a supernatural fire, and pride coursed through his veins. And, in truth, if vanity had ever been justifiable, it would indeed have been the vanity of Master Zacharius!

In fact, until he came along, the art of clockmaking had remained almost in its infancy. Since the day when Platon, four hundred years before the Christian era, invented the nocturnal clock, a type of clepsydra which marked the hours of the night with the sound of a flute playing, the science had remained almost unchanged. Masters worked on artistry rather than on mechanics, and it was the era of beautiful clocks made of iron, copper, wood, and silver, which were finely sculpted, like one of Cellini's ewers. One had a masterpiece of engraving, which measured time in a very imperfect way, but one had a masterpiece nevertheless. When the imagination of the artist was no longer focused on the perfection of the plastic arts, it strove to create those clocks with moving figurines, and with melodious chimes, whose stage setting was arranged in a greatly entertaining configuration. Besides, who was concerned, in that era, with regulating the flow of time? Legal limitation periods had not been invented; the physical and astronomical sciences had not based their calculations on rigorously precise measures; there were neither establishments closing at fixed hours, nor convoys departing on the second. Of an evening, the curfew time was sounded, and of a night, the hours were cried out in the midst of silence. Certainly, one did not live as long, if existence is measured by the quantity of matters conducted, but one lived better. The mind enriched itself on those noble sentiments born of contemplating masterpieces, and art was not created in a race. A church was built in two centuries; a painter produced but a few paintings in his life; a poet composed but one distinguished work, yet it was as many masterpieces as the centuries cared to appreciate.

When the precise sciences finally made some progress, clockmaking followed their development, despite the fact that it was always hindered by an insurmountable difficulty: the continuous and uniform measurement of time.

"You shall see that I have discovered the secrets..." (p. 18.)

Now, it was in the middle of this stagnation that Master Zacharius had invented the escapement, which allowed him to achieve a mathematical regularity by subjecting the pendulum's movement to a constant force. And this invention had gone to the old clockmaker's head. The pride, having risen in his heart, like mercury in a thermometer, reached the temperature of transcendental madness. By analogy, he had given himself over to materialistic consequences, and, in making his watches, he had believed himself to have caught the secrets of the union between the body and the soul unawares.

And so, on that day, seeing that Aubert was listening to him attentively, he said to him in a plain and convincing tone:

"Do you know what life is, my child? Have you comprehended the action of these springs that generate life? Have you looked into yourself? No, and yet, with the eyes of science, you would have seen the intimate connection that exists between the work of God and my own, for it is from his creation that I copied the arrangement of the cogs in my clocks."

"Master," replied Aubert sharply, "can you compare a machine made of copper and steel to the breath of God, the so-called soul, which animates the body, like the breeze imparts movement to the flowers? Could imperceptible cogs that make our arms and our legs move really exist? What parts could be so well calibrated that they could generate thoughts in us?"

"That is not the question," replied Master Zacharius softly, albeit with the stubbornness of a blind man walking toward an abyss. "To understand me, recall to mind the aim of the escapement that I invented. When I saw the irregularity in the workings of clocks, I understood that the movement contained in them was not sufficient, and that it was necessary to subject it to the regularity of another independent force. I therefore thought that the balance wheel could perform this function for me, if I managed to regulate its oscillations! Now, was it not a sublime idea, that which came to me, to make it restore the force it lost via the same clock movement that it was charged with regulating?"

Aubert made a sign of approval.

"Now, Aubert," continued the old clockmaker, becoming animated, "take a look at yourself! Do you, then, not understand that there are two distinct forces in us: that of the soul and that of the body, which is to say, a movement and a regulator? The soul is the source of life: therefore, it is the movement. Whether it is produced by a weight, by a spring, or by an intangible force, it is no less at the heart of it all. But, without the body, this movement would be uneven, irregular, and impossible! Consequently, the body comes to regulate the soul, and, like the balance wheel, it is subject to regular oscillations. Insomuch that one fares badly when eating, drinking, and sleeping, in a word, when the functions of the body are not properly regulated! Just like in my watches, the soul renders to the body the force lost through its oscillations. Eh, well! What then produces this intimate union of the body and the soul, if not a marvelous escapement, whereby the cogs of the one come to intermesh with the cogs of the other? Now, this is what I have divined, and applied, and there are no further secrets for me in this life, which is naught, after all, but an ingenious mechanism!"

Master Zacharius was a sublime sight in this state of delirium, which transported him right up to the last mysteries of infinity. But his daughter Gerande, standing at the threshold of the door, had heard everything. She rushed into her father's arms, and he held her convulsively to his chest.

"What is it, my daughter?" Master Zacharius asked her.

"If I had only a spring here," she said putting a hand on her heart, "I would not love you so much as I do, Father!"

Master Zacharius looked fixedly at his daughter and did not reply.

Suddenly, he gave out a cry, brought his hand quickly to his heart, and fell faint into his old leather armchair.

"Father! what is it?"

"Get help!" cried Aubert. "Scholastique!"

But Scholastique did not come running immediately. Somebody had struck the front door's door knocker. She had gone to open it, and, when she returned to the workshop, before she had opened her mouth, the old clockmaker, having regained his senses, said to her:

"I divine, Scholastique, my old girl, that you bring me still another one of these confounded watches which has stopped working!"

"Jesus! That is indeed the truth," replied Scholastique, handing a watch to Aubert.

"Father! what is it?" (p. 21.)

"My heart cannot be mistaken!" said the old man with a sigh.

And, despite the fact that Aubert wound the watch up with the greatest care, it no longer worked.

III.

A STRANGE VISIT.

Poor Gerande had watched as her life was extinguished along with her father's, not to mention Aubert, who anchored her to the world.

The old clockmaker was fading away little by little. His faculties were obviously tending toward deterioration, focusing on a single thought. Through a harmful association of ideas, he channeled everything into his monomania, and terrestrial life seemed to have withdrawn from him to make room for the supernatural life of intermediary powers. As a consequence, a few malicious rivals revived the diabolical rumors that had been spread about Master Zacharius' works.

The observation that his watches were afflicted with an inexplicable malfunctioning had a prodigious effect among the master clockmakers of Geneva. What did this sudden inertia of their cogs signify, and why the bizarre connections that they appeared to have with Master Zacharius' life? Therein lay such mysteries that one never considers without a secret terror. In the various classes of the city, from the apprentices right up to the lords who made use of the old clockmaker's watches, there was nobody who could not judge for himself the peculiarity of the facts. People tried to gain access to Master Zacharius, but to no avail. He himself fell very ill,—and this allowed his daughter to shield him from the incessant visits, which degenerated into reproaches and accusations.

The medicines and the doctors were powerless in relation to this organic decay, whose cause escaped them. It sometimes seemed that the old man's heart stopped beating, and then his heartbeats would resume with a disturbing irregularity.

It was customary, from that time onward, to submit the works of the master craftsmen to the judgement of the working class. The leaders of the different disciplines sought to distinguish themselves by the novelty and perfection of their works, and it was among them that Master Zacharius' condition received the most resounding pity, albeit a concerned pity. His rivals pitied him all the more willingly since they feared him less. They still remembered the old clockmaker's successes when he had exhibited his magnificent clocks with moving figurines, and his chiming watches, which had gained widespread admiration and demanded such high prices in the cities of France, Switzerland, and Germany.

However, thanks to the constant care of Gerande and Aubert, Master Zacharius' health appeared to improve a little, and in the midst of the tranquility that his convalescence afforded him, he managed to detach himself from the thoughts in which he had been absorbed. As soon as he could walk, his daughter led him out of the house, where the dissatisfied customers constantly abounded. Aubert himself remained in the workshop, pointlessly taking the rebellious watches apart and putting them back together again, and the poor boy, understanding none of it, at times clutched his head with his two hands, in fear of going mad like his master.

Gerande, meanwhile, guided her father's steps along the most pleasant promenades in the city. One afternoon, while supporting Master Zacharius' arm, she took in the Saint-Antoine Promenade, from where the view extends over the Cologny hillside and the lake. Occasionally, on beautiful mornings, one can see the gigantic peaks of Mount Buet standing on the horizon. Gerande called out by name all of these places which had been almost forgotten by her father, whose memory seemed to be muddled, and he himself experienced a childlike pleasure in learning all of these things, the memories of which had gone astray in his head. Master Zacharius leaned on his daughter, and their two heads of hair, one white and one blond, blended together in the same ray of sunshine.

It also came to pass that the old clockmaker finally realized that he was not alone in this world. Seeing his daughter, young and beautiful, himself old and broken, he considered that, after his death, she would remain alone, without support, and he looked around himself and around her. Many of the young craftsmen of Geneva had already courted Gerande; but none had gained access into the impenetrable refuge where the clockmaker's family lived. It was therefore only natural that, during this sunny spell in his mind, the old man's choice fell upon Aubert Thun. And once he had embarked on this train of thought, he observed that these two young people had been raised with the same ideas and the same beliefs, and that the oscillations of their hearts seemed to him to be "isochronal," as he said to Scholastique one day.

The old maidservant, literally enchanted by the word, even though she did not understand it, swore by her patron saint that the entire city would know about it within a quarter of an hour. Master Zacharius had great difficulty in calming her down, and finally managed to get her to keep her silence regarding this information, which she never did.

As a result, without Gerande and Aubert's knowledge, people throughout Geneva were already talking about their forthcoming union. However, it also transpired that, during these conversations, a peculiar snickering was often heard, along with a voice that said:

"Gerande will not marry Aubert."

If the interlocutors turned around, they found themselves facing a little old man whom they did not know.

How old was this peculiar being? Nobody could have said! It was conjectured that he must have existed for a great number of centuries, but that was all. His large squashed head sat on shoulders whose width equaled the height of his body, which was not more than three feet. His personage would have cut a handsome figure at the end of a pendulum rod, for a clockface would have fitted naturally over his face, and a pendulum would have oscillated at its ease in his chest. One could have readily taken his nose for the gnomon of a sundial, so thin and pointed it was; his teeth, spaced apart and shaped like epicycles, resembled the gears of a cogwheel and gnashed between his lips; his voice had the metallic sound of a bell, and one could hear his heart beat like the ticktock of a clock. This small man, whose arms moved like the hands on a clockface, walked along in fits and starts, without ever turning around. If he were followed, one found that he travelled at one league per hour and that his route was roughly circular.

This bizarre being had only been wandering like this, or rather, taking turns through the city, for a short while; but people had already noticed that, every day, just as the sun passed over the meridian, he came to a halt in front of Saint-Pierre's Cathedral, and then continued on his way after the twelve strikes of midday. Save for this precise moment, he seemed to appear suddenly in the middle of every conversation in which people were concerning themselves with the old clockmaker, and people wondered, with dread, what connection could exist between him and Master

Zacharius. In addition, people noticed that he did not let the old man and his daughter out of his sight during their leisurely strolls.

One day, on the Treille Promenade, Gerande noticed this monster, who was looking at her cheerfully. She pressed herself against her father in an act of fear.

"What is it, my Gerande?" asked Master Zacharius.

"I don't know," replied the young girl.

"I find you changed, my child!" said the old clockmaker. "There you have it, you're going to fall ill in your turn? Eh, well!" he added with a sad smile, "I shall have to take care of you, and take care of you well I shall."

"Oh! Father, it's nothing. I'm cold, and I suspect that it's…"

"Eh, what, Gerande?"

"The presence of that man who's following us endlessly," she replied in a low voice.

Master Zacharius turned around toward the little old man.

"My goodness, he is running well," he said with an air of satisfaction, "for it is exactly four o'clock. Fear not, my daughter, that's not a man, that's a clock!"

Gerande looked at her father in terror. How had Master Zacharius been able to read the time on the face of that strange creature?

"By the way," continued the old clockmaker, not concerning himself any further with this incident, "I haven't seen Aubert for a few days."

"Be that as it may, he hasn't left us, Father," replied Gerande, whose thoughts took on a softer tone.

"What's he doing, then?"

"He's working, Father."

"Ah!" exclaimed the old man, "he's working on repairing my watches, is it not so? But he will never manage it, for it is not repairs that they need, but rather resurrection!"

Gerande remained silent.

"I must know," added the old man, "whether or not anybody has as yet returned any more of those damned watches upon which the devil has cast an epidemic!"

Then, following these words, Master Zacharius fell into complete silence until the moment he knocked at the door of his house, and, for the first time since his convalescence, as Gerande returned sorrowfully to her room, he went down into his workshop.

Just as he went through the door, one of the numerous clocks hanging on the wall came to strike five o'clock. Ordinarily, the different chimes of these devices, which were admirably well-tuned, would sound simultaneously, and their concordance would delight the old man's heart; but, on this day, all of the bells chimed one after the other, so much so that for a quarter of an hour his ears were deafened by the successive sounds. Master Zacharius suffered terribly; he could not stand still, he went from one of these clocks to another, keeping time for them, like an orchestra conductor who was no longer master of his musicians.

When the last sound died out, the door of the workshop opened, and Master Zacharius shuddered from head to toe on seeing the little old man in from of him, who looked at him fixedly and said to him:

"Master, may I not speak with you for a moment?"

"Who are you?" asked the clockmaker brusquely.

"A colleague. It is I who is charged with regulating the sun."

"Ah! it's you who regulates the sun?" replied Master Zacharius sharply without blinking. "Eh, well! I can hardly compliment you! Your sun runs poorly, and, for us to reconcile with it, we are obliged either to turn our clocks forward or to turn them back!"

"And by the cloven foot of the devil!" exclaimed the monstrous personage, "you are correct, master! My sun does not always mark midday at the same moment as your clocks; but, one day, it shall be known that this is due to the irregularity of the Earth's translational motion, and a midday average will be invented which will regulate this irregularity!"

"Will I still be alive in that time?" asked the old clockmaker, whose eyes brightened.

"Without a doubt," replied the little old man cheerfully. "Do you really think that you will ever die?"

"Alas! I am nevertheless rather ill!"

"By the way, let's discuss that. By Beelzebub! that will lead us to that which I want to speak to you about."

And, saying this, the bizarre being jumped unceremoniously onto the old leather armchair and crossed his legs one under the other, like the scrawny crossbones that painters of funerary tapestries put beneath skulls. Then, he continued in an ironic tone:

"About that, Master Zacharius, what's going on, then, in this good city of Geneva? It is said that your health is deteriorating, and that your watches have need of doctors!"

He continued in an ironic tone... (p. 27.)

"Ah! you believe, do you, that there is an intimate connection between their lives and my own!" exclaimed Master Zacharius.

"I myself imagine that the watches have flaws, vices even. And if these hardy gadgets of yours are not functioning normally, then it is fair that they bear the punishment for their disorder. I am of the opinion that they require a little straightening up!"

"What are you calling flaws?" said Master Zacharius, blushing at the sarcastic tone with which these words had been uttered. "Do they not have the right to be proud of their origins?"

"Not so much, not so much!" replied the little old man. "They bear a famous name, and an illustrious signature is engraved on their clockfaces, it is true, and they have the exclusive privilege of being placed among the noblest families; but, lately, they have been malfunctioning, and you can do nothing about it, Master Zacharius, and the most unskilled of Geneva's apprentices would be able to show you a thing or two!"

"To help me, to help me, Master Zacharius!" cried the old man with a terrible burst of pride.

"To help you, Master Zacharius, who cannot bring your watches back to life!"

"But that's because I have a fever and they have one as well!" replied the old clockmaker, as a cold sweat ran down his every limb.

"Eh, well, they will die along with you, since you are so incapable of restoring a little elasticity to their springs!"

"Die! That cannot be, you have said so! I cannot die, not me, the foremost clockmaker in the world, not me who, by means of these various parts and cogs, knew how to regulate the movements with absolute precision! Have I not thusly subjected time to strict laws, and may I not dispose of it as its sovereign? Before such a sublime genius came to put these stray hours into order, what immense vagueness was human destiny plunged in? At what certain points in time could the acts of life be anchored to? But you, man or devil, whoever you are, have you ever even dreamed of the magnificence of my art, which calls all the sciences to its aid? No! No! I, Master Zacharius, I cannot die, since, because I regulated time, time shall end with me! It would return to that infinity from which my genius knew how to wrest it, and it would be irredeemably lost in the abyss of nothingness! No, I can no more die than can the Creator of the universe, which is subject to his laws! I have become his equal, and

I have shared in his power! If God created eternity, then Master Zacharius created time."

In that moment, the old clockmaker resembled a fallen angel, standing against the Creator. The little old man caressed him with his gaze, seemingly fanning the flames of all this impious rage.

"Well said, master!" he replied. "Beelzebub had less right than you to compare himself to God! Your glory must not perish! Therefore, I, your humble servant, would like to give you the means to tame those rebellious watches."

"What is it? what is it?" exclaimed Master Zacharius.

"You shall know it the day after the day on which you grant me your daughter's hand."

"My Gerande?"

"The one and the same!"

"My daughter's heart is not free," replied Master Zacharius to this demand, which did not appear to shock him nor to surprise him.

"Bah!... She is not the least beautiful of your clocks... but she, too, will end by stopping..."

"My daughter, my Gerande!... No!..."

"Eh, well! return to your watches, Master Zacharius! Take them apart and put them back together again! Arrange the wedding of your daughter and your apprentice! Quench springs made of your best steel! Bless Aubert and the beautiful Gerande, but remember that your watches will never work and that Gerande will not marry Aubert!"

And with that, the little old man left, but not so quickly that Master Zacharius failed to hear six o'clock strike in his chest.

IV.

THE CHURCH OF SAINT-PIERRE.

In the meantime, Master Zacharius' mind and body grew weaker and weaker. It was only extraordinary overexcitement that drew him back, more violently than ever, to his works of clockmaking, from which his daughter could no longer distract him.

His pride had increased all the more ever since his strange visitor had treacherously driven him into a state of hysteria, and he resolved to dominate, by the force of his genius, the confounded spell that hung over him and his works. He visited, first of all, the various clocks of the city entrusted to his care. With scrupulous attention to detail, he satisfied himself that the cogs were in good order, the pivots were sturdy, and the counterweights were perfectly balanced. There was not one part, right up to the chime bells, that he did not listen to with the reverence of a doctor examining a patient's chest. Nothing, then, indicated that these clocks were at the point of being struck down with inertia.

Gerande and Aubert often accompanied the old clockmaker on these visits. He himself must have taken pleasure in seeing them bustle about as they followed after him, and he certainly would not have been so preoccupied with his impending end if he had considered that his life force would be carried on by those of these cherished beings, and if he had understood that in children there always remains something of a father's life!

On returning home, the old clockmaker would take up his works again with feverish assiduity. Despite being convinced that he would not succeed, it nevertheless seemed to him impossible that this could be so, and he incessantly took apart and put back together all of the watches that people returned to his workshop.

Aubert, for his part, strove in vain to discover the cause of these troubles.

"Master," he said, "this can nevertheless be due only to the wearing of the pivots and the gears!"

"Do you take pleasure, then, in killing me with a thousand cuts?" replied Master Zacharius to him violently. "Are these watches the work of a child? Was it from fear of hurting my fingers that I stripped the surface off these pieces of copper with the lathe? Was it not to achieve a greater hardness that I forged them myself? Are these springs not quenched with a rare perfection? Can one use finer oils to dip them in? You yourself agree that that's impossible, and you must at last concede that the devil is somehow involved!"

Thereafter, from morning to night, the dissatisfied customers flooded into the house more than ever, and they made their way to the old clockmaker, who did not know which one to listen to.

"This watch is running slow and I cannot manage to regulate it!" said one customer.

"This one here," continued another, "is being very stubborn, and it has stopped moving, just as the sun stood still for Joshua!"

The dissatisfied customers flooded into the house... (p. 31.)

"If it is true that your health," repeated most of the dissatisfied customers, "has an influence on the health of your clocks, Master Zacharius, then get well as soon as possible!"

The old man looked at all of these people with wild eyes and responded with naught but nods of the head or rueful words:

"Wait until the first days of fair weather, my friends! That's the season when the life force in wearied bodies reignites! The sun must come along to warm us all up!"

"Oh, that's helpful, so our watches must be ill all winter long!" said one of the most furious customers to him. "Are you unaware, Master Zacharius, that your name is inscribed in full on their faces! By the Virgin! you do not do honor to your name!"

Eventually, it transpired that the old man, ashamed of these reproaches, took a few pieces of gold from his old chest and began to buy back the defective watches. At this news, the customers came running in droves, and the money reserves of this poor household quickly drained away; but the clock merchant's integrity remained intact. Gerande wholeheartedly applauded this tactfulness, which led directly to her ruin, and soon Aubert had to offer his savings to Master Zacharius.

"What will become of my daughter?" said the old clockmaker, at times grasping hold of, on this wreck, his feelings of paternal love.

Aubert did not dare to reply that he held high hopes for the future and felt greatly devoted to Gerande. Master Zacharius, on that day, might have even called him his son-in-law and refuted the baleful words which still buzzed in his ears:

"Gerande will not marry Aubert."

Nevertheless, using this system, the old clockmaker ended up ruining himself entirely. His old antique vases went off to foreign hands; he gave up magnificent oak panels, finely sculpted, which had adorned the walls of his home; soon a few naive paintings by the first Flemish painters no longer delighted his daughter's gaze, and everything, right up to the precious tools that he had invented with his genius, was sold to compensate the claimants.

Scholastique alone did not want to hear reason on such matters; but her efforts could not prevent the unwelcome visitors from getting in to see her master, nor from soon leaving again with some precious object. As a result, her chattering resonated in all the streets of the district, where she had long been well known.

She strove to refute the rumors of magic and sorcery which were circulating at Zacharius' expense; but since, deep down, she was convinced they were true, she said many prayers repeatedly to atone for her white lies.

It had been very well noted that the clockmaker had long since abandoned the observance of his religious duties. In times past, he had accompanied Gerande to the services and had appeared to find in prayer that intellectual charm with which it fills great minds, for it is the most sublime exercise of imagination. The old man's voluntary estrangement from holy practices, combined with the secretive habits of his existence, had, in some way, legitimized the accusations of sorcery which were made against his works. Therefore, with the dual purposes of bringing her father back to God and to the world, Gerande resolved to call religion to her aid. She thought that Catholicism could restore a little vitality to his dying soul; however, the dogmas of faith and humility were obliged to battle against the unconquerable pride in Master Zacharius' soul, and they clashed with that scientific hubris that ascribes everything to itself, without recourse to the infinite source from whence first principles emanate.

It was in these circumstances that the young girl undertook to convert her father, and her influence held such sway that the old clockmaker promised to attend High Mass at the cathedral the following Sunday. Gerande experienced a moment of ecstasy, as if the heavens had half opened before her eyes. Old woman Scholastique could not contain her joy and at last had irrefutable arguments against the malicious gossips who accused her master of impiety. She spoke about it to her neighbors, to her friends, to her enemies, and to those who knew her as equally as to those who did not know her at all.

"Good Lord, we can hardly believe what you're telling us, Scholastique," they replied to her. "Master Zacharius has always acted in concert with the devil!"

"Have you, then, not taken into account," continued the good woman, "the beautiful bell towers in which my master's clocks toll? How many times has he made the hours of prayer and Mass sound!"

"Undoubtedly," they replied to her. "But did he not invent machines which can walk of their own accord and which can do the work of a real man?"

"Could children of the devil," continued Scholastique in anger, "have managed to produce the beautiful iron clock at the Castle of Andernatt, which the city of Geneva was not rich enough to buy? Every hour, a beautiful aphorism appears on it, and a Christian who complied with it would go straight to paradise! Is that, then, the work of the devil?"

This masterpiece, made twenty years earlier, had indeed caused the glory of Master Zacharius to be praised to the skies; although, even on that occasion, accusations of sorcery had been common. Nevertheless, the return of the old man to the Church of Saint-Pierre would surely reduce the nasty gossips to silence.

Master Zacharius, no doubt forgetting the promise made to his daughter, returned to his workshop. After having seen that he was powerless to bring his watches back to life, he decided to try and see if he could not make new ones. He abandoned all those lifeless bodies and continued to work on finishing the crystal watch, which was to be his masterpiece; but no matter how hard he tried, making use of his finest tools, and using jewels and glass cutters which could withstand the friction, the watch broke apart in his hands the first time that he tried to assemble it!

The old man kept this incident a secret from everybody, even from his daughter; but from that moment on his life deteriorated rapidly. This was nothing other than the final oscillations of a pendulum which continue losing momentum when nothing comes to add to their original motion. It seemed that the laws of gravity, acting directly on the old man, were pulling him irresistibly toward the grave.

The Sunday so eagerly awaited by Gerande finally arrived. The weather was good and the temperature invigorating. The inhabitants of Geneva went calmly about the streets of the city, conversing cheerfully about the return of spring. Gerande, carefully taking the old man's arm, headed in the direction of Saint-Pierre's Cathedral, while Scholastique followed them carrying their books of hours. They were watched with curiosity as they went. The old man allowed himself to be led like a child, or rather, like a blind man. It was almost with a feeling of dread that the faithful of Saint-Pierre's Cathedral noticed him crossing the threshold of the church, and they even made to step back at his approach.

The hymns of High Mass were already ringing out. Gerande headed toward her customary bench and kneeled down in the most profound contemplation. Master Zacharius stayed close to her, standing.

The ceremonies of the Mass unfolded with the majestic solemnity of those faithful times, but the old man was not a believer. He did not beg for heaven's mercy with the mournful wails of the *Kyrie*; during the *Gloria in excelsis*, he did not sing the magnificence of the heavenly heights; the reading of the Gospel did not draw him out of his materialist reveries, and he forgot to join in with the Catholic homages of the *Credo*. The prideful old man remained motionless, insensitive and silent like a stone statue; and, at the solemn moment when the bell announced the miracle of transubstantiation, he didn't even bow down, and he looked directly at the divine Host which the priest raised above the faithful.

Gerande looked at her father, and heavy tears wetted her missal!

At that moment, the clock of Saint-Pierre struck half past eleven. Master Zacharius turned briskly around toward the old bell tower which was still ringing. It seemed to him as though the inner clockface were looking fixedly at him, as though the hour numerals were shining as if they had been engraved in strokes of fire, and as though the hands were throwing out electric sparks from their sharp points.

The Mass concluded. It was customary that the *Angelus* be recited at midday, and the officiants, before leaving the forecourt, waited for the hour to toll on the bell tower's clock. A few moments more, and the prayer would ascend to the feet of the Virgin.

But, suddenly, a shrill sound was heard. Master Zacharius gave out a cry...

The big hand on the clockface, having reached midday, suddenly stopped moving, and midday did not toll.

Gerande rushed to the aid of her father, who had been knocked over and was not moving, and whom they carried out of the church.

"This is the death blow!" said Gerande to herself, sobbing.

Master Zacharius, having been taken back to his house, was put to bed in a state of complete exhaustion. Life remained in him no longer, save for on the surface of his body, like the last clouds of smoke that waft around a recently extinguished lamp.

When he regained his senses, Aubert and Gerande were leaning over him. At this moment of reckoning, the future took the shape of the present in his eyes. He saw his daughter, alone, and without support.

The prideful old man... (p. 36.)

"My son," he said to Aubert, "I give you my daughter," and he extended his hand toward his two children, who were thereby united beside his deathbed.

But, suddenly, Master Zacharius sat up in a fit of rage. The words of the little old man returned to his mind.

"I don't want to die!" he cried out. "I cannot die! Me, Master Zacharius, I must not die... My books!... my accounts!..."

And, saying this, he darted out of his bed toward a book in which the names of his customers as well as the objects which he had sold to them were recorded. He flicked through the book with greed, and his scrawny finger came to rest on one of the pages.

"Here!" he said, "here!... This old iron clock, sold to this Pittonaccio! It's the only one which has not yet been returned to me! It exists! it works! it still lives! Ah! I want it! I shall find it! I shall take such good care of it that death shall no longer have a hold on me."

And then he fainted.

Aubert and Gerande kneeled down by the old man's bed and prayed together.

V.

THE HOUR OF DEATH.

A few more days passed by, and Master Zacharius, this man who was almost dead, got out of his bed and returned to life, driven by supernatural overexcitement. He was living on pride. However, Gerande was not mistaken: her father's body and soul were forever lost.

The old man was then seen to be busy mustering his remaining resources, without showing any concern for his family. He expended an incredible amount of energy, marching around, rummaging about, and muttering mysterious words.

One morning, Gerande went down into his workshop. Master Zacharius was not there. All day long, she waited for him. But Master Zacharius did not return.

Gerande cried out all the tears in her eyes, but her father did not reappear.

Aubert went about the city and learned the sorry fact that the old man had left Geneva.

"Let's find my father!" exclaimed Gerande when the young apprentice reported the distressing news to her.

"Where could he be?" Aubert asked himself.

A flash of inspiration suddenly lit up his mind. Master Zacharius' last words came back to him. The old clockmaker was no longer living, save for in the old iron clock which had not been returned to him! Master Zacharius must have set out to find it.

Aubert explained his thinking to Gerande.

"Let's take a look at my father's book," she replied to him.

They both went down into the workshop. The book was open on the workbench. All of the watches and clocks that the old clockmaker had made, and which had been returned to him as a result of their malfunctioning, had been erased, except for one!

"Sold to Lord Pittonaccio, one iron clock, with chimes and moving figurines, delivered to his Castle of Andernatt."

This was the "moral" clock of which old woman Scholastique had spoken with such praise.

"That's where my father is!" exclaimed Gerande.

"Let's hurry there," replied Aubert. "We can still save him!..."

"Not for this life," whispered Gerande, "but at least for the next!"

"By God's good graces, Gerande! The Castle of Andernatt is located in the gorges of the Teeth of Midday Mountains, about twenty hours from Geneva. Let's go!"

That very evening, Aubert and Gerande, followed by their old maidservant, walked on foot along the road that runs alongside Lake Geneva. They travelled five leagues during the night, stopping neither at Bessinge, nor at Ermance, where the famous Castle of Mayor stands. They waded across the torrents of the River Dranse with no small difficulty. Everywhere they went they inquired about Master Zacharius, and they were soon certain that they were following in his footsteps.

The following day at nightfall, after having passed Thonon, they reached Evian, from where one can see the view of Switzerland's coast as it stretches out over an expanse of twelve leagues. But the two betrotheds did not even notice these enchanting sites. They continued on, driven by a supernatural force. Aubert, supporting himself with a knotty stick, offered his arm at times to Gerande and at times to old woman Scholastique, and he tapped into a supreme energy within his heart in order to support his companions. The three of them spoke of their sorrows, and their hopes, and in this manner followed the beautiful road by the shoreline, along the narrow plateau which joins the banks of the lake with the high mountains of Chalais. Soon they reached Bouveret, at the place where the Rhone flows into Lake Geneva.

On leaving that town, they left the lake behind, and their fatigue increased in the midst of these mountainous lands. Vionnaz, Chesset, Collombay, somewhat isolated villages, soon stood behind them. However, their knees were weakened, and their feet were mangled by the sharp ridges which protruded from the ground like bushes of granite. There was no trace of Master Zacharius!

They had to find him nevertheless, and the two betrotheds sought rest neither at isolated cottages, nor at the Castle of Monthey, which, along with its dependencies, comprised the domain of Marguerite de Savoie. Finally, toward the end of the day, almost dying of fatigue, they reached the Hermitage of Notre-Dame of Sex, which is located at the base of the Tooth of Midday peak, six hundred feet above the Rhone.

The hermit received the three of them at nightfall. They could not have gone one step further, and here they had to get some rest.

The hermit had no news of Master Zacharius for them. They could hardly hope to find him alive in the midst of these gloomy solitudes. The night was dark, the storm whistled in the mountains, and avalanches rushed down from the summit of trembling rocks.

The two betrotheds, huddling in front of the hermit's hearth, recounted to him their harrowing story. Their coats, steeped in snow, were drying in a corner, and, outside, the dog of the hermitage let out lugubrious barks, which combined with the howling of the gale.

"Pride," said the hermit to his guests, "has lost an angel created for the good. It is the stumbling block upon which the destinies of man stumble. Against pride, the origin of all the vices, one cannot put forward any reasoning, since, by its very nature, the prideful refuse to hear it... There is therefore nothing more to do but pray for your father!"

The four of them kneeled down, just as the dog's barking redoubled, and somebody knocked on the door of the hermitage.

"Open up, in the name of the devil!"

The door gave way under violent efforts, and there appeared a disheveled man, haggard, and barely clothed.

"Father!" cried Gerande.

It was Master Zacharius.

"Where am I?" he said. "In eternity!... Time has stopped... the hours strike no more... the hands have stopped!"

"Father," continued Gerande with such heartbreaking emotion that the old man appeared to return to the world of the living.

"You're here, my Gerande!" he cried, "and you, Aubert!... Ah! my dear betrotheds, you have come to get married at our old church!"

"Father," said Gerande, seizing him by the arm, "return to your house in Geneva, come back with us!"

The old man broke free from his daughter's grip and dashed toward the door, on the threshold of which large snowflakes were piling up.

"Do not abandon your children!" cried Aubert.

"Why," replied the old clockmaker sadly, "why return to those places which my life has already left, and where a part of myself is buried forevermore!"

"Your soul is not dead!" said the hermit in a deep voice.

"My soul!... Oh! no!... its cogs are in good order!... I can feel it beating at regular intervals..."

"Your soul is immaterial! Your soul is immortal!" continued the hermit forcefully.

"Yes... like my glory!... But it is locked away in the Castle of Andernatt, and I want to see it again!"

The hermit crossed himself. Scholastique was almost inanimate. Aubert supported Gerande in his arms.

"The Castle of Andernatt is inhabited by a damned soul," said the hermit, "a damned soul who does not salute my hermitage's cross!"

"Father, don't go there!"

"I want my soul! my soul belongs to me..."

"Hold him back! hold my father back!" cried Gerande.

But the old man had already crossed the threshold and dashed out into the night, shouting:

"Help me! help me, my soul!..."

Gerande, Aubert, and Scholastique rushed after him. They treaded along impracticable paths, along which Master Zacharius went like a storm, driven by an irresistible force. The snow whirled around them and intermixed its white flakes with the foam of the overflowing torrents.

As they passed the chapel erected in memory of the massacre of the Theban Legion, Gerande, Aubert, and Scholastique promptly crossed themselves. Master Zacharius was not there.

At last, in the midst of this uncultivated region, the village of Evionnaz appeared. The most hardened heart would have been moved at the sight of this isolated township in the midst of these horrible solitudes. But the old man took no notice. He headed to the left, and he plunged into the deepest gorges of the Teeth of Midday Mountains, which bite at the sky with their pointed peaks.

Before long, a ruin, old and dark like the rocks at its base, towered before him.

"There it is! there!..." he cried, once again hurrying along on his wild course.

The Castle of Andernatt, in that era, was already nothing more than ruins. A wide tower, worn down, and falling to pieces, towered over it and seemed to threaten the old gables which rose at its base with its collapse. These enormous piles of stones were horrible to see. One got the impression that, in the midst of the clutter, there were gloomy rooms with collapsed ceilings, and foul receptacles full of vipers.

A low and narrow postern, opening onto a pit filled with rubble, gave access into the Castle of Andernatt. What occupants had passed through here? nobody really knew. No doubt, some margrave, half brigand, half lord, had sojourned in this residence. That margrave had been succeeded by bandits or counterfeiters, who had been hung at the scene of their crimes. And legend had it that, on winter's nights, Satan came to conduct his traditional sarabands on the slopes of the deep gorges which swallowed up the shadows of the ruins!

Master Zacharius was not frightened by their sinister appearance. He reached the postern. Nobody prevented him from passing. A large and tenebrous courtyard appeared before his eyes. Nobody prevented him from crossing it. He climbed a kind of inclined plane which lead to one of the long corridors whose arches seemed to crush the daylight beneath their heavy footings. Nobody opposed his passage. Gerande, Aubert, and Scholastique continued to follow him.

Master Zacharius appeared to be sure of his way and walked at a rapid pace, as if he were being guided by an invisible hand. He arrived at an old worm-eaten door which eased open beneath his blows, while bats flew in oblique circles around his head.

"There it is! there!..." (p. 42.)

A huge hall, better preserved than the others, presented itself to him. Tall carved panels covered the walls, on which larvae, ghouls, and tarasques seemed to stir confusedly. A few windows, long and narrow, similar to murder holes, rattled under the discharges of the storm.

Master Zacharius, having reached the middle of the hall, gave out a cry of joy.

On an iron stand placed by the wall sat the clock in which his entire life force now resided. This unequalled masterpiece depicted an old Roman church, with its buttresses of forged iron and its hefty bell tower, which housed a complete set of chimes for the antiphon of the day, the Angelus, the Mass, the Vespers, the Compline, and the Benediction. Above the door of the church, which opened at service times, a rose window had been made, at the center of which moved two hands, and its archivolt, engraved in relief, replicated the twelve hours of the clockface. Between the door and the rose window, just as old woman Scholastique had described it, different maxims, relevant to the activities of each part of the day, appeared on a copper panel. In former times, Master Zacharius had arranged this succession of aphorisms with a wholly Christian conscientiousness; the hours of prayer, work, repast, recreation, and rest followed each other according to religious doctrine, and were infallibly bound to greet conscientious observers with their recommendations.

Master Zacharius, drunk with joy, went to seize this clock, when a hideous laugh erupted behind him.

He turned around, and, in the light of a smoky lamp, he recognized the small old man from Geneva.

"You here!" he cried.

Gerande was frightened. She pressed herself up against her betrothed.

"Hello, Master Zacharius," said the monster.

"Who are you?"

"Lord Pittonaccio, at your service! You have come to give me your daughter! You remembered my words: Gerande will not marry Aubert."

The young apprentice hurled himself at Pittonaccio, who eluded him like a shadow.

"Stop, Aubert!" said Master Zacharius.

"Good night," said Pittonaccio, who vanished.

"Father," cried Gerande, "let's flee this accursed place!... Father!..."

But Master Zacharius was no longer there. He was chasing Pittonaccio's phantom up and down the collapsing levels of the castle. Scholastique, Aubert, and Gerande remained, devastated, in the huge hall. The young girl fell into a stone armchair; the old maid-servant kneeled down next to her and prayed. Aubert remained standing to watch over his betrothed. Pale glimmers of light twisted in the shadows, and the silence was interrupted only by the work of those small animals which eat away at antique timbers and whose sound marks time on "death's clock."

By the first rays of daylight, the three of them ventured up and down the endless staircases which ran around beneath this heap of stones. For two hours, they wandered around like this without encountering a living soul, and heard nothing but distant echoes responding to their calls. At times, they found themselves buried one hundred feet underground, at other times, they dominated the heights of the wild mountains.

Chance finally led them back to the vast hall which had sheltered them during their night of anxiety. It was no longer empty. Master Zacharius and Pittonaccio were there talking together, one standing, stiff like a corpse, the other crouching on a marble table.

Master Zacharius, having noticed Gerande, went to take her by the hand and lead her toward Pittonaccio saying:

"Here is your master and lord, my daughter! Gerande, here is your husband!"

Gerande shuddered from head to toe.

"Never!" exclaimed Aubert, "for she is my betrothed."

"Never!" replied Gerande, like a plaintive echo.

Pittonaccio took to laughing.

"Do you want my death, then?" cried the old man. "Here, in this clock, the last one that still works, of all those which have left my hands, herein my life force is locked away, and this man says to me: 'Once I have your daughter, this clock shall belong to you.' And this man does not want to wind it up! He can break it and cast me into nothingness! Ah! my daughter! you would then love me no more!"

"Father!" whispered Gerande, coming to her senses.

"If only you knew how I have suffered being so far away from this source of my life force!" continued the old man. "Perhaps this clock has not been well taken care of! Perhaps its springs have been left to wear out, its cogs left to seize up! But now, with my own hands, I am going to maintain its health, which is so very dear to me, for it must not be that I die, not me, the great clockmaker of Geneva! Look, my daughter, how its hands move around at a steady rate! Look, now five o'clock is about to toll! Listen closely, and look at the beautiful maxim that shall appear before your eyes."

Five o'clock tolled on the clock's bell tower with a sound that resounded woefully in Gerande's soul, and these words appeared in red letters:

One must eat the fruits of the tree of knowledge.

Aubert and Gerande looked at each other in astonishment. This was no longer one of the Catholic clockmaker's orthodox aphorisms! The breath of Satan must have passed through here. Master Zacharius took no further notice of it, and he continued:

"Do you hear that, my Gerande? I live, I still live! Listen to my breathing!... Look at the blood flowing in my veins!... No! you would not wish to kill your father, and you will accept this man as your husband, so that I may become immortal, and so that I may at last attain the power of God!"

At these impious words, old woman Scholastique crossed herself, and Pittonaccio gave out a roar of joy.

"And then, Gerande, you shall be happy with him! Look at this man, he is Time! Your life will be regulated with absolute precision! Gerande! I gave life to you, give life back to your father!"

"Gerande," whispered Aubert, "I am your betrothed!"

"He's my father!" replied Gerande, collapsing in a heap.

"She is yours!" said Master Zacharius. "Pittonaccio, you will keep your promise!"

"Here is the key to the clock," replied the horrible personage.

Master Zacharius grabbed the long key, which resembled an uncoiled grass snake, and he ran to the clock, which he began to wind up with fantastical speed. The grinding of the spring was nerve-rattling. The old clockmaker continued winding and winding, his arm didn't stop moving, and it seemed that this movement of rotation was independent of his volition. He wound like this, faster and faster and in strange contortions, until he collapsed from fatigue.

"There you have it, it's wound up for a century!" he cried.

Aubert exited the hall like a madman. After numerous detours,

"Look at this man, he is Time!" (p. 46.)

he found his way out of the accursed residence and dashed into the countryside. He returned to the hermitage of Notre-Dame of Sex, and he spoke to the holy man with such desperate words that the man agreed to go with him to the Castle of Andernatt.

If, during these hours of anxiety, Gerande did not cry, it was because her eyes had already run out of tears.

Master Zacharius did not leave the vast hall. Every passing minute, he listened to the steady beating of the old clock.

Meanwhile, ten o'clock tolled, and, to Scholastique's great horror, these words appeared on the silver clockface:

Man can become God's equal.

Not only was the old man no longer shocked by these impious maxims, but he read them with rapture and reveled in these prideful thoughts while Pittonaccio circled around him.

The marriage contract was due to be signed at midnight. Gerande, almost inanimate, no longer saw or heard anything. The silence was only interrupted by the old man's words and Pittonaccio's snickering.

Eleven o'clock tolled. Master Zacharius shuddered, and, with a resounding voice, read this blasphemy:

Man must be a slave of science,
and for it sacrifice relations and family.

"Yes," he cried out, "there is naught but science in this world!"

The hands slithered over the iron clockface with snakelike hisses, and the clockwork movement ticked with hurried beats.

Master Zacharius spoke no more! He had fallen to the ground, he groaned, and from his breathless chest came only these broken words:

"Life! science!"

The scene then had two new witnesses: the hermit and Aubert. Master Zacharius was lying on the ground. Gerande, close to him, more dead than alive, prayed...

Suddenly, the sharp snap which precedes the tolling of the hour was heard.

Master Zacharius sat up straight.

"Midnight," he cried.

He was dead. (p. 50.)

The hermit extended his hand toward the old clock... and midnight did not strike.

Master Zacharius then let out a scream which must have been heard from hell, when these words appeared:

Whoever dares to make himself God's equal
will be damned for eternity!

The old clock exploded with the sound of lightning, and the spring, breaking loose, bounded across the hall in a thousand fantastical contortions. The old man stood up and ran after it, seeking in vain to grab hold of it and crying out:

"My soul! my soul!"

The spring bounced ahead of him, going from one side to the other, without him managing to seize it!

At last, Pittonaccio grabbed hold of it, and, uttering a terrible blasphemy, he was swallowed up into the earth.

Master Zacharius fell over backward. He was dead.

. . . .

The body of the old clockmaker was buried amid the peaks of the Andernatt. Aubert and Gerande then returned to Geneva, and, during the long years that God granted them, they endeavored to redeem the soul of the condemned man of science with prayer.

I.

There were seven or eight hundred of them there, at the very least. Of medium size, but strong, agile, flexible, made for prodigious leaps, they gamboled beneath the last glimmers of the sun, which was setting beyond the mountains spread out toward the west of the bay. The reddish disk soon disappeared, and darkness began to creep into the middle of the basin, which was surrounded by the faraway sierras of Sanorra, Ronda and the sorry land of Cuervo.

Suddenly, the whole troop stood still. Its leader had just appeared on the ridge of the mountain, which forms a skinny donkey's back. From the military base, perched at the far end of the enormous rock, nothing that took place beneath the trees could be seen.

"Sriss!... Sriss!" sounded the leader, his lips, protruding in a pout, gave this hiss an extraordinary intensity.

"Sriss!... Sriss!" the strange troop repeated in perfect unison.

A singular being, this leader was, of tall stature, dressed in a monkey skin, fur on the outside, his head was a tangle of unkempt hair, his face bristled with a short beard, and his bare feet were tough underneath like the hooves of a horse.

He raised his right arm and pointed it toward the lower ridge of the mountain. The whole troop immediately repeated this movement with military precision, it is more accurate to say mechanical precision,—veritable marionettes powered by the same spring. He lowered his arm. They lowered their arms. He crouched down to the ground. They crouched down in the same position. He picked up a sturdy stick which he brandished. They brandished their sticks and waved them like windmills the same as him,—like the windmills which baton twirlers call "the covered rose."

Then, the leader turned around, slipped between the bushes, and crawled along under the trees. The troop followed him, crawling along.

In less than ten minutes, the pathways of the mountain, furrowed by the rains, had been traversed without the dislodgement of a single stone which could have indicated the presence of this mass on the march.

A quarter of an hour later, the leader stopped. The troop stopped as if it had been frozen in place.

Two hundred meters below, the town appeared, lying alongside the dark harbor. Numerous lights studded the indistinct clusters of jetties, houses, villas, and barracks. Beyond them, the lamps of the warships, and the lights of the merchant ships and the pontoons, lying at anchor, reflected off the surface of the calm waters. Farther along, at the extremity of Europa Point, the lighthouse projected its bright beam out into the strait.

At that moment, a cannon blast exploded, the *First Gunfire*, fired from one of the razing batteries. And then, the rumble of drums, accompanied by the sharp whistle of fifes, sounded immediately thereafter.

It was the hour of retirement, the hour to return home. No longer did any foreigner have the right to move around the town without being escorted by an officer from the garrison. The crews were ordered to return aboard before the doors were closed. Every quarter of an hour, patrols circulated to escort the latecomers and drunkards back to their posts. Then, everything was silent.

General Mac Kackmale could sleep soundly.

It did not seem as though England had anything to fear, on this night, concerning its Rock of Gibraltar.

II.

We know all about it, this formidable rock, four hundred and twenty-five meters high, lying on a base twelve hundred and forty-five meters wide, four thousand three hundred meters long. It somewhat resembles an enormous sleeping lion, the head facing toward Spain, the tail dipping into the sea. Its face shows its teeth,—seven hundred cannons pointing out from its embrasures,—the *Old Woman's Teeth*, as they say. An old woman who would bite hard if she were irritated. As such, England is securely stationed here, like at Perin, at Aden, at Malta, at Pulau Pinang, at Hong Kong, so many rocks which, someday, with the progress of mechanics, she will transform into revolving fortresses.

In the meantime, Gibraltar assures the United Kingdom of incontestable dominion over the eighteen kilometers of the strait, which the club of Herakles opened up between Abila and Calpe, at the very edge of Mediterranean waters.

Have the Spaniards given up retaking this piece of their peninsula? Yes, without a doubt, since it seems to be unassailable by land or by sea.

However, there was one man who was haunted by the obsessive thought of reconquering this offensive and defensive rock. He was the leader of the band, a strange being, one could even say a madman. This hidalgo was precisely named Gil Braltar, a name which, in his thinking no doubt, predestined him for this patriotic conquest. His brain had not resisted the thought, and his lot, in different circumstances, would have been life in an insane asylum. He was well known. And yet, for ten years, not much was known of what had become of him. Perhaps he was wandering around the world? In reality, he had not left his ancestral land. Here he lived the existence of a troglodyte, in the woods, in grottoes, and most particularly, in the depths of the inaccessible recesses in San-Miguel's Cave, which, it is said, flow into the sea. He was believed to be dead. And yet, he lived, albeit like a savage man, devoid of human reason, who obeys nothing more than animal instincts.

"Surrender!" he cried. (p. 57.)

III.

He was sleeping quite soundly, General Mac Kackmale, longer than regulations required. With his disproportionately long arms, his round eyes, sunken beneath bushy eyebrows, his face framed with a rough beard, his grimacing physiognomy, his anthropopithecus-like gestures, and the extraordinary prognathism of his jaw, he was remarkably ugly,—even for an English general. A real ape, and an excellent serviceman besides, despite his simian form.

Yes! He slept in his comfortable residence on Main Street, that winding road which traverses the town from the Sea Gateway to the Alameda Gateway. Perhaps he was dreaming that England was seizing Egypt, or Turkey, or Holland, or Afghanistan, or Sudan, or the Boer states, in a word, all the points of the globe at her convenience,—and this at the moment when she risked the loss of Gibraltar.

The door to the room opened abruptly.

"What is it?" asked General Mac Kackmale, sitting up with a start.

"My general," replied an aide-de-camp who had just entered like a torpedo shell, "the town's being invaded!..."

"The Spanish?..."

"I believe so!"

"They have dared!..."

The general did not finish. He stood up, threw aside the madras which was tied around his head, rolled into his pants, dove into his dress coat, slid into his boots, put his hat on his head, and buckled on his sword, all the while saying:

"What's that sound that I hear?"

"The sound of chunks of rock rolling like an avalanche into the town."

"Are there many of the scoundrels?..."

"There must be."

"Have all the bandits of the coast now united, no doubt for this raid: those smugglers from Ronda, the fishermen from San-Roque, and the refugees who swarm in the villages?..."

"That is the fear, my general!"

"And has the governor been informed?"

"No! It's impossible to get to him at his Europa Point villa! The

They all went back up the slopes of the mountain. (p. 60.)

gateways are occupied, and the roads are packed with assailants!..."

"And the barracks at the Sea Gateway?..."

"There's no way to get there! The artillerymen must be surrounded in their barracks!"

"How many men do you have with you?..."

"Twenty or so, my general, infantrymen from the 3rd Regiment who were able to escape."

"By Saint Dunstan!" cried Mac Kackmale, "Gibraltar snatched from England by these orange sellers!... This shall not be!... No! This shall not be!"

At that moment, the door to the room gave passage to a strange being who jumped onto the general's shoulders.

IV.

"Surrender!" he cried in a hoarse voice, which sounded more like a roar than a human voice.

A few men, rushing behind the aide-de-camp, went to throw themselves at this man, when, in the brightness of the room, they recognized him.

"Gil Braltar!" they cried.

It was him indeed, the hidalgo whom nobody had thought of for a long time, the savage of San-Miguel's Cave.

"Surrender?" he yelled.

"Never!" replied General Mac Kackmale.

Suddenly, at the moment when the soldiers surrounded him, Gil Braltar gave out a shrill and prolonged "sriss."

Immediately, the courtyard of the residence, then the residence itself, was filled with a swarming mass...

Would anyone believe it? It was apes, it was monkeys, and by the hundreds! Had they now come to take back from the English this rock of which they are the true owners, this mountain that they occupied well before the Spanish, well before Cromwell had dreamed of its conquest for Great Britain? In truth, yes! And they were formidable in their numbers, these tailless monkeys, which one lives with harmoniously only on the condition that their thievery is tolerated, these intelligent and audacious beings whom one is wary of upsetting, since they take revenge—this had happened a few times—by rolling enormous rocks into the town!

And now, these monkeys had become the soldiers of a madman, as savage as them, of this Gil Braltar whom they knew well, who lived their independent life, of this quadrumanified William Tell, whose entire existence centered on this thought: to drive the foreigners out from Spanish territory!

What a disgrace for Great Britain if the attempt succeeded! The English, conquerors of the Hindus, the Abyssinians, the Tasmanians, the Australians, the Hottentots, and so many others, conquered by simple monkeys!

If such a catastrophe occurred, then General Mac Kackmale would have nothing left to do but blow off his own head. One does not survive such a dishonor!

However, before the monkeys, called by the hissing of their leader, had invaded the room, a few soldiers had managed to throw themselves at Gil Braltar. The madman, endowed with an extraordinary vigor, resisted, and it was not without difficulty that they managed to subdue him. His borrowed skin having been torn from him in the struggle, he remained almost naked in a corner, bound, gagged, and unable to move or to make himself heard. A short time later, Mac Kackmale dashed out of his house, determined to conquer or die, in accordance with the military expression.

But the danger was no less great outdoors. Surely, a few infantrymen must have managed to rally at the Sea Gateway and were marching toward the general's residence. Several gunshots rang out in Main Street and in Market Square. All the same, the number of monkeys was such that the garrison of Gibraltar soon risked being forced to cede the place to them. And then, if the Spanish made common cause with these monkeys, the forts would be abandoned, the batteries would be deserted, the fortifications would no longer count a single defender, and the English, who had rendered this rock impregnable, would no longer be able to retake it.

Suddenly, a reversal occurred.

Indeed, by the light of a few torches which lit up the courtyard, the monkeys could be seen beating a retreat. At the head of the band marched their leader, brandishing his stick. All of them, imitating the movements of his arms and legs, followed him with the same gait.

So, had Gil Braltar been able to break free from his bonds, to escape from the room where they had been keeping him? It could no longer be doubted. But where was he going now? Was he going to head toward Europa Point, to the governor's villa, to attack him, to demand that he surrender, like he had done with regard to the general?

No! The madman and his band went down Main Street. Then, after having passed the Alameda Gateway, they all took off obliquely across the park and went back up the slopes of the mountain.

One hour later, not a single one of Gibraltar's invaders remained in the town.

So, what had happened?

It was soon known, when General Mac Kackmale appeared at the edge of the park.

It was he who, taking the place of the madman, had lead the retreat of the band after having enveloped himself in the prisoner's monkey skin. He very much resembled a quadrumane, this brave warrior, who had deceived the monkeys themselves. Consequently, all he had had to do to get them to follow after him was to appear!...

Quite simply a genius idea, which was soon rewarded with the bestowal of the Saint George Cross.

As for Gil Braltar, the United Kingdom handed him over, in exchange for cash, to a Barnum who makes his fortune parading him through the major cities of the Old and New Worlds. He even readily leads people to believe, this Barnum, that it's not the savage from San-Miguel's Cave whom he exhibits, but General Mac Kack-male in person.

However, this adventure has been a lesson for the government of Her Gracious Majesty. It has understood that if Gibraltar cannot be taken by men, then it is at the mercy of monkeys. Consequently, England, being very practically minded, has decided from now on to send only the ugliest of its generals, so that the monkeys may continue to be deceived.

This measure, in all likelihood, forever assures it possession of Gibraltar.

A DRAMA IN THE AIR.

In the month of September 185–, I arrived in Frankfurt on the Main. My passage through Germany's major cities had been splendidly interspersed with a number of aerostatic ascents; but, to date, no inhabitant of the Confederation had accompanied me in my basket, and the fine experiments conducted in Paris by Messieurs Green, Eugene Godard, and Poitevin had still not managed to persuade the serious Germans to attempt the aerial routes.

However, news of my next ascent had barely begun to spread around Frankfurt when three prominent citizens requested the favor of coming with me. We were to lift off from Comedy Square two days thereafter. I then immediately occupied myself with readying my balloon. It was made of silk treated with gutta-percha, a substance which is impervious to acids and gasses, and which is totally waterproof, and it had a volume—three thousand cubic meters—which allowed it to ascend to the greatest heights.

The day of the grand September Fair, which brings large crowds into Frankfurt, was the day set for the liftoff. The town gas, of a perfect quality and having a strong upward force, had been provided to me in excellent condition, and, toward eleven o'clock in the morning, the balloon had been filled up, but only to three quarters, an indispensable precaution, since, as one goes higher, the layers of the atmosphere diminish in density, and the fluid, trapped within the bands of the balloon, acquires more elasticity and could tear the walls. My calculations had provided me with exactly the quantity of gas required to carry my companions and me.

We were set to depart at midday. The spectacle of the impatient crowd which thronged around the cordoned-off area, flooding the entire square, pouring into the surrounding streets, and lining the houses on the square from the ground floors to the slate gables, was a magnificent sight. The strong winds of the previous days had fallen silent. An oppressive heat bore down from the cloudless sky. Not a breath of air disturbed the atmosphere. With weather such as this, one could land at the same place from which one had taken off.

I brought along three hundred pounds of ballast, divided into sacks; the basket, entirely round, which was four feet in diameter and three feet deep, was comfortably furnished; the hemp net which supported it stretched symmetrically around the upper hemisphere of the hot-air balloon; the compass was in place, the barometer was suspended on the ring which tied all the support ropes together, and the anchor was carefully attached. We were ready to depart.

Among the people who thronged around the cordoned-off area, I noticed a young man with a pale face and anxious features. The sight of him struck me. He was a diligent spectator of my ascents whom I had already encountered in a number of German cities. With an anxious look, he gazed avidly at the strange flying machine, which remained immobile a few feet from the ground, and he remained silent amid all the other spectators.

Midday sounded. This was the moment. My traveling companions did not appear.

I sent word to each of their homes and I learned that one had left for Hamburg, another for Vienna, and the third for London. Their hearts had failed them at the moment of undertaking one of these excursions which, thanks to the skillfulness of today's aeronauts, are devoid of any danger. As they were, in some way, part of the festival program, they had been seized by the fear that they would be obliged to carry it out faithfully, and they had fled far away from the theater at the moment when the curtain rose. Their courage was obviously equal to the inverse ratio of the square of their speed... to make a run for it.

The crowd, half disappointed, displayed considerable ill humor. I had no hesitation in lifting off alone. In order to reestablish the equilibrium between the specific gravity of the balloon and the weight which had to be lifted, I replaced my companions with new sacks of sand and I got into the basket. The twelve men who restrained the aerostat with twelve ropes fastened to the equatorial ring let them pass between their fingers a little, and the balloon rose a few feet from the ground. There was not a single puff of wind, and the atmosphere, weighing down like lead, seemed impassible.

"Is everything ready?" I shouted.

The men readied themselves. A final glance told me that I could lift off.

"Look out!"

There was some kind of movement in the crowd, which seemed to me to breach the cordoned-off area.

"Release the ropes!"

The balloon rose slowly, but I was struck by a blow which knocked me down to the bottom of the basket.

When I regained my feet, I found myself face-to-face with an unexpected passenger, the young pale man.

"I bid you hello, monsieur!" he said to me with grand composure.

"With what right…?"

"Am I here?… With the right that is given to me by the impossibility, with which you're now faced, of sending me back!"

I was stunned. This aplomb disconcerted me, and I had nothing to reply.

I stared at this intruder, but he took no notice of my surprise.

"Is my weight disturbing your equilibrium, monsieur?" he said. "Allow me…"

And, without waiting for my consent, he unballasted the balloon of two sacks which he threw into space.

"Monsieur," I then said, taking the only stand possible, "you are here…, fine! you will stay… fine!… but to me alone belongs the right to fly the aerostat…"

"Monsieur," he replied, "your urbanity is very French. It comes from the same country as me! I figuratively shake the hand that you refuse me. Take your measures and do as you see fit! I shall wait until you have finished…"

"To…?"

"To chat with you."

The barometer had fallen to twenty-six inches. We were at a height of approximately six hundred meters above the city; but nothing betrayed the horizontal displacement of the balloon, since the mass of air surrounding it moves along with it. A sort of hazy heat bathed the objects spread out beneath our feet and lent to their contours a regrettable blurriness.

I looked at my companion once more.

He was a man of about thirty years, simply clothed. The sharp edges of his features revealed an indomitable spirit, and he appeared to be very muscular. Due entirely to the surprise with which this silent ascent had struck him, he remained motionless, trying to distinguish the objects which blended together in the vague scene.

"What annoying haze!" he said after a few moments.

"I bid you hello, monsieur!" he said to me. (p. 63.)

I did not reply.

"You're mad at me!" he continued. "Bah! I couldn't pay for this trip, I rather had to jump aboard by surprise."

"Nobody is asking you to get out, monsieur!"

"Eh! did you not know, then, that the same thing happened to the counts of Laurencin and Dampierre, when they took off from Lyon, on 15 January 1784. A young merchant named Fontaine climbed onto the gondola, at the risk of capsizing the flying machine!... He completed the journey, and nobody died!"

"Once we are back on the ground, we shall discuss this further," I replied, stung by the light tone with which he spoke to me.

"Bah! let's not think about returning!"

"Do you think, then, that I will delay descending?"

"Descending!" he said with surprise. "Descending!—Let's begin, first of all, by ascending."

And, before I could prevent him, two sacks of sand had been thrown out of the basket, without even having been emptied!

"Monsieur!" I cried out in anger.

"I know of your skillfulness," replied the stranger calmly, "and your majestic ascents have caused a stir. But if experience is the sister of practice, then she is in some way the cousin of theory, and I have made an extensive study of the aerostatic art. This has gone to my head!" he added sadly, falling into silent contemplation.

The balloon, after having risen again, became stationary.

The stranger consulted the barometer and said:

"Here we are at eight hundred meters! The people look like insects. Look! It's from this height, I think, that they should always be studied, so as to judge their proportions soundly! Comedy Square has been transformed into a gigantic anthill. Look at the crowd as it crams the quays, and Zeil Street as it gets smaller. We're above the Cathedral. The River Main is already nothing more than a whitish line cutting through the city, and that bridge, the Main Bridge, looks like a wire cast between the two banks of the river."

The atmosphere had cooled a little.

"There's nothing that I wouldn't do for you, my host," my companion said to me. "If you are cold, then I shall take off my clothes and I shall lend them to you."

"Thank you!" I replied dryly.

"Bah! Necessity dictates law. Give me your hand, I am your

"Monsieur!" I cried out in anger. (p. 65.)

fellow countryman, you shall educate yourself in my company, and my conversation will compensate you for the troubles that I have caused you!"

I sat myself down, without replying, at the opposite end of the basket. The young man had taken a bulky notebook out from his greatcoat. It was a study on aerostation.

"I possess," he said, "the most curious collection of engravings and caricatures which have been made regarding our aerial mania. Oh, how we have simultaneously admired and scorned this precious invention! We are fortunately no longer in the age when the Montgolfier brothers attempted to make artificial clouds with steam, and to manufacture a gas with electrical properties, which they produced by burning wet straw and wool clippings."

"Do you wish, then, to diminish the merit of inventors?" I replied, "because I have played my part in this venture. Is it not magnificent to have proved by experiment the possibility of rising into the air?"

"Eh! monsieur, who is denying the glory of the first aerial navigators? They had to have immense courage to take off by means of these rather fragile envelopes, which contain only heated air! But, I ask you, has the aerostatic science not now made giant leaps since the ascents of Blanchard, which is to say, within around about a century? Look here, monsieur!"

The stranger took an engraving out from his collection.

"Here," he said to me, "this is the first aerial voyage undertaken by Pilatre de Rosiers and the marquis d'Arlandes, four months after the invention of balloons. Louis XVI refused to give his consent for the voyage, and, instead, two men condemned to death were supposed to be the first to attempt the aerial routes. Pilatre de Rosiers was indignant at this injustice, and, by way of intrigue, he managed to set off. They had still not invented this basket which makes maneuvering easy, and, instead, a circular gondola ran around the lower and narrower part of the hot-air balloon. The two aeronauts thus each had to stay on opposite sides of the gondola without shifting around because the wet straw with which it was filled restricted all movement. A flaming stove was suspended beneath the opening of the balloon; when the voyagers wanted to rise, they threw straw onto this blaze, at the risk of setting the flying machine alight, and the heated-up air gave a new upward force to the balloon. The two daring navigators departed, on 21 November 1783, from the Muette gardens, which the dauphin had put at their disposal. The aerostat rose majestically, flew along the Ile of Cygnes, crossed the River Seine at the Conference Customhouse, and, heading between the dome of the Invalids' Hotel and the Military School, it approached Saint-Sulpice Church. The aeronauts then added fuel to the fire, crossed the boulevard, and descended beyond the Enfer Customhouse. On touching down, the balloon crumpled, and, for a few moments, buried Pilatre de Rosiers beneath its folds!"

"What an unfavorable omen!" I said, interested in these details, which were close to my heart.

"An omen of the catastrophe which would, later on, cost the life of that unfortunate soul!" replied the stranger sadly. "Have you never experienced something similar?"

"Never."

"Bah! misfortunes often come without warning!" added my companion.

And he remained silent.

Nevertheless, we were advancing toward the south, and Frankfurt had by now fled beneath our feet.

"Maybe we shall encounter that thunderstorm," said the young man.

"We shall descend before that," I replied.

"Well, I never! It would be better to ascend! We shall evade it more surely."

And two new sacks of sand went over the side into space.

The balloon rose rapidly and stopped at twelve hundred meters. A rather brisk cold made itself felt, despite the rays of sunshine, which fell on the envelope and dilated the gas inside it, giving it a greater upward force.

"Fear not," the stranger said to me. "We have three thousand five hundred toises of breathable air. In any event, do not concern yourself with what I'm doing."

I wanted to stand, but a firm hand nailed me to my seat.

"What's your name?" I asked.

"My name? What is it to you?"

"I am asking you for your name!"

"My name is Herostratos or Empedokles, the choice is yours."

This response was not reassuring in the least.

The stranger, moreover, spoke with a cold-bloodedness which

was so singular that I asked myself, not without concern, with whom I was dealing.

"Monsieur," he continued, "nobody has dreamed up anything new since the physicist Charles. Four months after the invention of aerostats, and that skillful man had invented the valve which allows the gas to escape when the balloon is too full, or when one wants it to descend; and the basket, which facilitates the maneuvers of the flying machine; the net, which holds the envelope of the balloon and distributes the load across its entire surface; the ballast, which allows for the balloon to rise and for the landing site to be chosen; the rubber coating, which makes the fabric waterproof; and the barometer, which indicates the height attained. Lastly, Charles used hydrogen, which, fourteen times lighter than air, allows for the highest layers of the atmosphere to be reached and does not expose one to the dangers of an aerial combustion. On 1 December 1783, three hundred thousand spectators crammed around the Tuileries Palace. Charles lifted off, and the soldiers presented arms to him. He traveled nine leagues in the air, flying his balloon with a skillfulness which the aeronauts of today have not surpassed. The king endowed him with a pension of two thousand livres, because, at that time, new inventions were encouraged!"

The stranger then appeared to me to be in the grip of a certain agitation.

"Myself, monsieur," he continued, "I have studied the matter and I am convinced that the first aeronauts actually steered their balloons. Not mentioning Blanchard, whose assertions may be dubious, Guyton de Morveau, with the aid of oars and a rudder, endowed his flying machine with noticeable movements and a marked direction. Recently, in Paris, a clockmaker, Monsieur Julien, conducted convincing experiments at the Racetrack, in which, thanks to a particular mechanism, his flying machine, shaped like an oblong, was manifestly steered against the wind. Monsieur Petin has thought up the idea of juxtaposing four hydrogen balloons and, by means of tapered sails arranged horizontally, he hopes to obtain a change in the equilibrium which, when inclining the aircraft, will endow it with a sideways motion. People often speak of engines destined to overcome the resistance of the air currents, the propeller, for example; but the propeller, operating in a moving environment, will not provide a solution. I, monsieur, I myself have discovered the only way to steer balloons, and not one learned society has come to my aid, not one city has filled my subscription lists, not one government has wanted to hear me! It's villainous!"

The stranger thrashed about while gesticulating, and the basket experienced violent oscillations. I had great difficulty in bringing it under control.

Nevertheless, the balloon had encountered a faster air current, and we were advancing toward the south, at a height of fourteen hundred meters.

"There's Darmstadt," my companion said to me while leaning over the side of the basket. "Can you see its castle? Not clearly, wouldn't you say! But what can you do? The heat from the storm is making the shapes of objects waver, and you need a keen eye to recognize the localities!"

"Are you certain that it's Darmstadt?" I asked.

"Without a doubt, and we are six leagues from Frankfurt."

"Then we must descend!"

"Descend! You're not suggesting that we descend onto the church towers?" said the stranger, chuckling.

"No, but in the environs of the city."

"Eh, well! let's avoid the church towers!"

While saying this, my companion grabbed the ballast sacks. I rushed at him; but he knocked me down with one hand, and the unballasted balloon reached two thousand meters.

"Stay calm," he said, "and don't forget that Brioschi, Biot, Gay-Lussac, Bixio and Barral went to even greater heights to conduct their scientific experiments."

"Monsieur, we must descend," I continued, trying to coax him gently. "The storm is forming around us. It would not be wise..."

"Bah! We shall go higher than it, and we shall cease to fear it!" cried my companion. "What's more glorious than dominating these clouds which overwhelm the earth! Is it not an honor to navigate along the aerial streams like this? The grandest personages have journeyed like us. The marquise and the countess of Montalembert, the countess of Podenas, Mademoiselle La Garde, and the marquis of Montalembert took off from the suburb of Saint-Antoine, headed for these unknown shores, and the duke of Chartres displayed considerable skill and presence of mind during his ascent on 15 July 1784. In Lyon, the counts of Laurencin and Dampierre; in Nantes, Monsieur de Luynes; in Bordeaux, d'Arbelet des Granges; in Italy, the knight, Andreani; and from our era, the duke of Brunswick, have all left the tracks of their glory in the air. To equal those grand personages, we must go even higher into the celestial reaches than them! To approach infinity is to comprehend it!"

The rarefaction of the air dilated the hydrogen in the balloon considerably, and I saw its lower part, left empty on purpose, begin to swell, making a release of the valve imperative; but my companion did not seem determined to allow me to maneuver as I pleased. I resolved, therefore, to secretly pull on the valve rope while he spoke with animation, for I feared to divine with whom I was dealing! That would have been too horrible! It was around a quarter to one. It had been forty minutes since we had left Frankfurt, and from the south, driving against the wind, came thick clouds ready to clash with us.

"Have you lost all hope of making your schemes succeed?" I asked with interest... keenly interested.

"All hope!" replied the stranger dully. "Wounded by the refusals, and the mockery, these low blows have finished me off! This is the eternal torture reserved for innovators! Look at these caricatures from every era with which my wallet is filled!"

While my companion flicked through his papers, I seized the valve rope, without him realizing it. It was to be feared, however, that he would notice the sound of the hissing, like a waterfall, which the gas makes while escaping.

"Nothing but jokes were made about Father Moilan!" he said. "He was obliged to take off with Janninet and Bredin. During the mission, their hot-air balloon caught fire, and the ignorant rabble tore it to pieces! Then the satirical cartoon *Curious Animals* called them *Mewing Jean Minet* and *The Scoundrel.*"

I pulled on the valve rope, and the barometer began to rise again. It was time! A few faraway thunderclaps rumbled to the south.

"Look at this other engraving," continued the stranger, without suspecting my maneuvers. "It's a huge balloon carrying a ship, fortresses, and houses, etc. The caricaturists did not think that their silliness would one day become a reality! It's fully loaded, this large vessel; on the left, its rudder, with the living quarters of the pilots; at the prow, holiday houses, a gigantic organ and a cannon to attract the attention of the inhabitants of the earth or the moon; above the stern, the observatory and the launch balloon; at the equatorial ring, the living quarters of the army; on the left, the headlamp, then the upper balconies for strolling, the sails, and the ailerons; beneath, the cafes and the general food supplies store. Behold this magnificent advertisement: 'Invented for the happiness of mankind, this orb will soon depart for the ports of the Levant, and, on its return, it will announce its voyages for the two poles as well as for the far reaches of the West. There is no need to worry about a thing; everything has been provided for, everything will go like clockwork. There will be an exact fare for all of the stopover destinations, and the prices will be the same for the regions which are the farthest removed from our hemisphere; namely: one thousand louis for any one of the aforementioned voyages. And one could say that this amount is very modest, with regard to the speed, the convenience, and the pleasures which one shall enjoy in the aforementioned aerostat, pleasures that one does not encounter here below, whereas in this balloon everyone shall find their fantasies brought to life. Insomuch that, in the same space, some will be dancing, others will be at ease; some will dine on delicacies and others will fast; whoever would like to converse with witty people will find somebody to speak with; whoever is carefree will not lack an equal. Thus, pleasure shall be the soul of aerial society!' All of these inventions were met with laughter… But before long, if my days are not numbered, we shall see that these projects in the air become a reality!"

We were visibly descending. He didn't notice it!

"And take a look at this variety of balloon game," he continued, spreading out in front of me some of the engravings, of which he had a considerable collection! "This game contains the entire history of the aerostatic art. It is for the use of elevated minds, and is played with dice and tokens for the agreed stakes, which one pays or collects, depending on the square one lands on."

"Well," I continued, "you seem to have studied the science of aerostation intensively?"

"Yes, monsieur! yes! From the time of Phaethon, from the time of Ikaros, from the time of Archytas, I've researched everything, consulted everything, learned everything! Through me, the aerostatic art would render great services to the world, if God were to lend me life! But that shall not be!"

"Why?"

"Because my name is Empedokles or Herostratos!"

Fortunately, however, the balloon got closer to the ground; although, when one falls, the danger is just as bad at one hundred feet as at five thousand!

"Do you recall the battle of Fleurus?" continued my companion, whose face became more and more animated. "It was at that battle that Coutelle, by order of the government, organized a company of balloonists! At the siege of Maubeuge, General Jourdan gained such utility from this new mode of observation that, twice a day, and with the general himself, Coutelle lifted off into the air. Communication between the aeronaut and the balloonists, who restrained the balloon, was effected by means of small white, red, and yellow flags. Often rifle and cannon shots were fired at the aircraft at the moment when it lifted off, but without result. When Jourdan was preparing to surround Charleroi, Coutelle traveled close to the area, lifted off from the Jumet plain, and remained in observation with General Morlot for seven or eight hours, which doubtlessly contributed to us gaining victory at Fleurus. And, as a matter of fact, General Jourdan praised the assistance that he received from the aeronautical observations very highly. Eh, well! despite the services rendered on that occasion and during the Belgian campaign, the year which saw the military career of balloons begin also saw it end! And the Meudon School, founded by the government, was closed by Bonaparte on his return from Egypt! And yet, as Franklin said, what is expected of a child which has just been born? If the child was born viable, it must not be suffocated!"

The stranger put his head in his hands and took to thinking for a few moments. Then, without raising his head, he said to me:

"Despite my best efforts, monsieur, you have opened the valve?"

I let go of the rope.

"Fortunately," he continued, "we still have three hundred pounds of ballast!"

"What are your intentions?" I then said.

"Have you never traversed the seas?" he asked me.

I felt myself turn pale.

"It is regrettable," he added, "that we are being blown toward the Adriatic Sea! It's nothing but a stream! But, higher up, perhaps we shall find other air currents?"

And, without looking at me, he unballasted the balloon of a few sacks of sand. Then, in a menacing voice:

"I allowed you to open the valve," he said, "because the dilation

"He remained in observation for seven or eight hours." (p. 73.)

of the gas threatened to burst the balloon! But don't try that again!"

And he continued in these terms:

"You must know all about the crossing from Dover to Calais made by Blanchard and Jefferies! It was magnificent! On 7 January 1785, driven by a north-west wind, their balloon was inflated with gas by the Dover coast. A miscalculation of equilibrium, when they had barely taken off, forced them to jettison their ballast so as not to fall again, and they retained only thirty pounds. It wasn't enough, for the wind didn't freshen, and they made but slow progress toward the French coast. Moreover, the permeability of the fabric made the aerostat deflate little by little, and, after an hour and a half, the voyagers realized that they were descending.

" 'What should we do?' said Jefferies.

" 'We're only three quarters of the way there,' replied Blanchard, 'and not very high! If we go higher, perhaps we shall encounter more favorable winds.'

" 'Let's jettison the rest of the sand!'

"The balloon regained a little upward force, but it was not long before it descended again. Toward the halfway point of the journey, the aeronauts got rid of the books and tools. A quarter of an hour later, Blanchard said to Jefferies:

" 'What of the barometer?'

" 'It's increasing! We are lost, and yet the French coast is right there!'

"A loud noise sounded."

" 'Has the balloon torn?' said Jefferies.

" 'No! the loss of gas has deflated the lower part of the balloon! But we are still descending! We're lost! Overboard with all nonessential items!'

"The provisions, the oars, and the rudder were thrown into the sea. The aeronauts were at a height of no more than one hundred meters.

" 'We are rising again,' said the doctor.

" 'No, it's the momentum caused by the decrease in weight! And there's not a ship in sight, not a bark on the horizon! Into the sea with our clothes!'

"The poor wretches stripped off, but the balloon continued to descend!

" 'Blanchard,' said Jefferies, 'you must make this journey alone; you agreed to bring me along; I shall sacrifice myself! I'm going to throw myself into the water, and the unburdened balloon will rise again!'

" 'No, no! that's dreadful!'

"The balloon deflated more and more, and its concavity, forming a parachute, pushed the gas against the walls and increased the leakage!

" 'Goodbye, my friend!' said the doctor. 'May God save you!'

"He was going to throw himself overboard, when Blanchard held him back.

" 'One recourse is left to us!' he said. 'We can cut the ropes which hold the basket and hang on to the netting! Perhaps the balloon will recover itself. Let's get ready! But... the barometer is descending! We're rising! The wind is freshening! We're saved!'

"The voyagers sighted Calais! They were delirious with joy! A few moments later, they crashed down in the Guines Forest."

"I have no doubt," added the stranger, "that in the same circumstances, you would follow doctor Jefferies' example!"

The clouds rolled in dazzling masses before our eyes. The balloon cast large shadows on the bank of clouds and was shrouded as if by a halo. Thunder rumbled beneath the basket. It was all terrifying!

"Let's descend!" I cried.

"Descend, when the sun is there, waiting for us! Overboard with the sacks!"

And the balloon was unballasted of more than fifty pounds!

At three thousand five hundred meters, we became stationary. The stranger talked incessantly. I was completely dejected, while he, it seemed, was living in his element.

"With a good wind, we could go far!" he cried. "In the Antilles, there are air currents which travel at one hundred leagues an hour! At Napoleon's coronation, Garnerin launched a balloon illuminated with colored glass, at eleven o'clock in the evening. The wind was blowing from the north-north-west. The next day at daybreak, the inhabitants of Rome greeted its passage above the dome of Saint Peter's Basilica! We shall go even farther... and even higher!"

I barely heard! Everything whirred around me! A gap appeared in the clouds.

"Look at that city!" said the stranger. "It's Speyer!"

I leaned out of the basket and I saw a small black heap. It was Speyer. The River Rhine, so wide, resembled an unrolled ribbon.

"The balloon deflated more and more." (p. 76.)

Above our heads, the sky was a dark azure. The birds had long since abandoned us, since, in this rarefied air, their flight would have been impossible. We were alone in space, and I was in the company of the stranger!

"It's not necessary for you to know where I'm taking you," he then said, and he threw the compass into the clouds. Ah! it's a beautiful thing, a free fall! You're surely aware that, from the time of Pilatre de Rosiers right up to the time of Lieutenant Gale, there have been few victims of aerostation, and that the misfortunes which have occurred are always due to recklessness. Pilatre de Rosiers took off with Romain, from Boulogne, on 13 June 1785. He had suspended a hot-air balloon from his gas balloon, in order to overcome, no doubt, the need to release gas or jettison ballast. It was like putting a stove beneath a powder keg! The fools reached four hundred meters and were carried by opposing winds, which tossed them over the open sea. To descend, Pilatre wanted to open the aerostat's valve, but the valve rope got caught on the balloon and tore it so much that it deflated in an instant. He fell onto the hot-air balloon, making it wheel around and carry away the unfortunate souls, who were smashed to pieces in a few seconds. It's horrifying, is it not?"

I could only reply with these words:

"For pity's sake! let's descend!"

The clouds wrapped around us from all sides, and terrifying detonations, which reverberated in the cavity of the aerostat, erupted all around us.

"You are making me impatient!" cried the stranger, "and you shall no longer know if we are rising or if we are descending!"

And the barometer went overboard to join the compass, along with a few sacks of earth. We must have been at a height of five thousand meters. A few icicles had already formed on the sides of the basket, and a sort of fine snow chilled me to the bone. And yet, the terrible thunderstorm was raging beneath our feet, but we were higher than it.

"Have no fear," the stranger said to me. "It is only fools who become victims. Olivari, who perished at Orleans, took off in a hot-air balloon made of paper; his basket, suspended beneath the stove and ballasted with combustible materials, was consumed by the flames; Olivari fell and died! Mosment took off from Lille on a light platform; and a buffeting made him lose his equilibrium; Mosment fell and died! Bittorf, at Manheim, saw his balloon made of paper go up in flames in the air; Bittorf fell and died! Harris took off in a badly constructed balloon, whose valve was too big and could not be shut off; Harris fell and died! Sadler, deprived of ballast from his long stay in the air, was carried over the city of Boston and crashed into the chimneys; Sadler fell and died! Coking descended with a convex parachute which he claimed to have perfected; Coking fell and died! Eh, well, I love them, these victims of their own recklessness, and I shall die like them! Higher! higher!"

All the ghosts of this necrology flashed before my eyes! The rarefaction of the air and the rays of the sun increased the dilation of the gas, and the balloon continued to rise! I automatically attempted to open the valve, but the stranger cut the rope a few feet above my head... I was lost!

"Did you see Madame Blanchard fall?" he said to me. "I saw it, me! yes, me! I was at the Tivoli gardens on 6 July 1819. Madame Blanchard took off in a balloon of small size, to save on the cost of filling it, and she was obliged to inflate it fully. Consequently, the gas leaked from the lower appendage, leaving in its path a veritable trail of hydrogen. She took with her, suspended from beneath the basket by an iron cable, a type of halo firework that she was going to set alight. She had repeated this experiment many times. And on that day, she took off with a small parachute ballasted with a firework that terminated in a ball of silver rain. She was going to launch this device, after having set it alight with a fire lance made specially for the purpose. She took off. The night was dark. At the moment of lighting her firework, she was careless enough to swing the fire lance beneath the stream of hydrogen which was spewing out of the balloon. My eyes were fixed on her. All of a sudden, an unexpected glow lit up the darkness. I thought it was a surprise from the clever aeronaut. The glow grew brighter, disappeared suddenly, and reappeared at the top of the aerostat in the form of a huge jet of flaming gas. That sinister brightness illuminated the boulevard and the entire district of Montmartre. Then, I saw the poor wretch get up, twice attempt to close off the appendage of the balloon to extinguish the fire, then sit in the basket and attempt to guide her descent, since she hadn't fallen out. The combustion of the gas lasted for several minutes. The balloon, shrinking more and more, continued descending, but it wasn't free-falling! The wind was blowing from the north-west and tossed it over Paris.

There, in the vicinity of the house at No. 16 De Provence Road, there were vast gardens. The aeronaut could fall into them without any danger. But alas, it was fate! The balloon and the basket crashed into the roof of the house! The impact was soft. 'Help!' cried the unfortunate soul. I arrived at the road at that moment. The basket slid across the roof and got caught on an iron spike. At that jolt, Madame Blanchard was thrown out of her basket and dashed onto the pavement. Madame Blanchard was killed!"

These stories froze me with horror! The stranger was on his feet, bareheaded, with ruffled hair, and wild eyes!

Delusion was no longer possible! I finally saw the horrible truth! I was dealing with a madman!

He jettisoned the rest of the ballast and we must have been carried to a height of at least nine thousand meters! Blood came out of my nose and my mouth!

"What is there that's more glorious than martyrs of science?" the madman then cried. "They are canonized by posterity!"

But I no longer heard. The madman looked around himself and kneeled down by my ear:

"And the catastrophe of Zambecarri, have you forgotten it? Listen. On 7 October 1804, the weather appeared to clear a little. On the preceding days, the wind and the rain had not ceased, but the ascent announced by Zambecarri could not be postponed. His enemies were already ridiculing him. He was obliged to take off in order to save himself and science from public ridicule. This was at Bologna. Nobody helped him to fill his balloon.

"It was at midnight that he lifted off, accompanied by Andreoli and Grossetti. The balloon rose slowly, as it had been perforated by the rain and the gas was leaking. The three intrepid voyagers could see the barometer reading only with the aid of a dark lantern. Zambecarri had not eaten in twenty-four hours. Grossetti also had an empty stomach.

" 'My friends,' said Zambecarri, 'the cold has seized me, I'm exhausted. I'm going to die!'

"He fell unconscious on the gondola. The same happened to Grossetti. Andreoli alone stayed awake. After repeated attempts, he managed to shake Zambecarri from his numbness.

" 'Have there been any developments? Where are we going? Which direction is the wind coming from? What time is it?'

" 'It's two o'clock!'

" 'Where is the compass?'

" 'Overboard!'

" 'Good God! the candle in the lantern has gone out!'

" 'It can no longer burn in this rarefied air,' said Zambecarri!

"The moon had not risen, and the atmosphere was saturated with a horrible gloom.

" 'I'm cold, I'm cold! Andreoli. What are we to do?'

"The poor wretches descended slowly through a layer of whitish clouds.

" 'Shh!' said Andreoli. 'Do you hear that?'

" 'What?' replied Zambecarri.

" 'That rather particular sound!'

" 'You must be mistaken!'

" 'No!'

"Can you imagine those voyagers, in the middle of the night, listening to that incomprehensible sound! Would they crash into a tower? Would they be dashed onto rooves?

" 'Do you hear that? It sounds like the sound of the sea!'

" 'Impossible!'

" 'It's the roaring of waves!'

" 'It's true!'

" 'Light the lantern! light the lantern!'

"After five fruitless attempts, Andreoli managed to light the lantern. It was three o'clock. The sound of the waves sounded violently. They were almost touching the surface of the sea!

" 'We are lost!' cried Zambecarri, and he grabbed a big sack of ballast.

" 'Help us!' cried Andreoli.

"The basket touched the water, and the waves came up to their chests!

" 'Into the sea with the instruments, the clothes, and the money!'

"The aeronauts stripped off everything. The unballasted balloon rose with terrifying speed. Zambecarri suffered a severe bout of vomiting. Grossetti bled profusely. The poor wretches were so short of breath that they couldn't speak. The cold seized them, and, within moments, they were covered in a layer of ice. The moon appeared to them to be red like blood.

"After traveling through these high regions for a half hour, the flying machine fell into the sea once again. It was four o'clock in the morning. The castaways had half of their bodies in the water,

"His balloon got caught on a tree, and his lamp set it alight." (p. 83.)

and the balloon, making sail, dragged them along for several hours.

"At daybreak, they found themselves facing Pesaro, four miles from the coast. They were going to reach it, when a gust of wind tossed them back into the open sea.

"They were lost! The terrified barks fled at their approach!... Fortunately, a more experienced sailor drew up alongside them, hauled them aboard, and they disembarked at Ferrada.

"A terrifying voyage, was it not? But Zambecarri was an energetic and brave man. Barely having recovered from his ordeal, he resumed his ascents. During one of them, he crashed into a tree, and his spirits of wine lamp spilled onto his clothes; he was covered in flames, and his flying machine was set ablaze, just as he was able to touch down, half scorched!

"Lastly, on 21 September 1812, he attempted another ascent at Bologna. His balloon got caught on a tree, and his lamp set it alight once again. Zambecarri fell and died!

"And in full knowledge of these facts we would still hesitate! No! The higher we go, the more glorious death shall be!"

The balloon having been completely unballasted of all the objects that it had contained, we were carried to unfathomable heights. The aerostat vibrated in the atmosphere. The slightest sound made the celestial vault ring out. Our terrestrial globe, the only object which struck my eye in the vastness of space, seemed ready to vanish, and, above us, the heights of the star-studded sky receded into endless darkness!

I saw the singular being draw himself up in front of me!

"Now is the time!" he said to me. "We must die! We have been rejected by mankind! They despise us! Let's vanquish them!"

"Have mercy!" I said.

"Let's cut the ropes! May this basket be abandoned in space! The attractive force will change direction, and we shall reach the sun!"

Despair galvanized me. I threw myself at the madman, we grabbed each other, and a horrifying struggle took place! But I was knocked down, and, while he pinned me under his knee, the madman cut the basket's ropes.

"One!..." he said.

"My God!..."

"Two!... three!..."

I made a superhuman effort, I recovered myself and repelled the madman violently!

The madman disappeared into space! (p. 85.)

"Four!" he said.

The basket fell, but, instinctively, I clung to the ropes and hoisted myself into the meshing of the net.

The madman disappeared into space!

The balloon was carried to an immeasurable height! There was a horrible crack!... The gas, too dilated, had burst the envelope! I closed my eyes...

A few moments later, a humid heat revived me. I was surrounded by clouds on fire. The balloon whirled with a terrifying vertigo. Carried by the wind, it traveled at one hundred leagues an hour on its horizontal path, and lightning bolts crisscrossed all around it.

However, my fall was not very fast. When I reopened my eyes, I saw the countryside. I was two miles from the sea, and the storm was pushing me along with force when a sudden jolt made me release my grip. My hands opened, a rope slipped rapidly between my fingers, and I found myself on the ground!

It was the anchor rope, which, sweeping the surface of the land, had gotten caught in a crevice, and my balloon, unballasted one last time, was lost beyond the seas.

When I came to, I was in a bed at a peasant's house, in Harderwick, a small town in Guelders, fifteen leagues from Amsterdam, on the banks of the Zuyderzee.

A miracle had saved my life, but my voyage was nothing more than a series of reckless actions, carried out by a madman, which I could not have guarded against!

May this terrible story, in instructing those who read it, not at all discourage explorers of the aerial routes!

TEXTUAL NOTE.

The source texts used for the translations of "Master Zacharius" and "A Drama in the Air" were "Maître Zacharius" and "Un drame dans les airs" in Jules Verne's *Le Docteur Ox* published by J. Hetzel et Cie. in 1874. This was the first book edition in which these stories appeared. An earlier version of "Master Zacharius" was originally published in two parts under the title "Maître Zacharius : ou l'Horloger qui avait perdu son âme" in the illustrated periodical literary magazine *Musée des familles : Lectures du soir* in April and May of 1854. An earlier version of "A Drama in the Air" was originally published under the title "Un voyage en ballon" in the *Musée des familles : Lectures du soir* in August of 1851.

The source text used for the translation of "Gil Braltar" was "Gil Braltar" in Jules Verne's *Le Chemin de France* published by J. Hetzel et Cie. in 1887. This was the first book edition in which the story appeared. The story was also published in the newspaper *Le Petit Journal : Supplément du dimanche* in January of that same year.

Both *Le Chemin de France* and *Le Docteur Ox* were published as part of the Extraordinary Journeys series during Jules Verne's lifetime and represent the standard French editions of these works. The illustrations which accompany the translations are from these same book editions.

GLOSSARY OF UNCOMMON WORDS.

MASTER ZACHARIUS.

antiphon: a short liturgical verse that is sung or spoken at religious services.

archivolt: a decorative carving or molding around an arch.

book of hours: a book containing prayers and other religious texts to be recited at the canonical hours of the day.

clepsydra: an ancient water clock.

convalescence: a period of recovery from illness.

epicycle: the curve produced by rolling a small circle around a larger circle while tracing out the path of a fixed point on the small circle.

ewer: a jug or pitcher.

firebrand: a piece of burning wood.

galliot: a small, flat-bottomed sailboat.

gnomon: the raised or projecting part of a sundial that casts a shadow onto the dial.

isochronal: occurring at regular time intervals.

loquacity: talkativeness.

margrave: a princely title from the Holy Roman Empire, similar to "lord."

missal: a book containing liturgical texts used at religious services.

murder hole: a small hole in a ceiling through which weapons can be fired or scalding liquids can be poured.

officiant: a person who conducts religious services, such as a priest.

pile: a pole or post driven into a riverbed that supports an overlying structure.

postern: a side door or back door; or a side gate or back gate.

promenade: a public pathway where people can take leisurely strolls.

receptacle: a vessel or container in which things are kept.

repast: a meal or mealtime.

saraband: a slow, stately court dance.

solitude: an isolated or lonely place.

tarasque: a mythological dragon creature.

Teeth of Midday Mountains: "Dents-du-Midi" in original French.

GIL BRALTAR.

anthropopithecus: an obsolete taxonomic term for the chimpanzee species.

embrasure: an opening or porthole in a wall or other fortified structure through which weapons are fired.

fife: a small flute.

madras: a piece of cotton fabric, often colored or patterned, worn around the head as a headscarf.

prognathism: a lower jaw or chin that juts forward.

quadrumane: a primate whose four feet can be manipulated like hands.

quadrumanify: to transform into a quadrumane, see *quadrumane*.

simian: having to do with monkeys or being like a monkey.

A DRAMA IN THE AIR.

aerostat: a hot-air balloon or blimp or other lighter-than-air flying machine.

aerostatics: the study of air and other gasses in states of mechanical equilibrium.

aerostation: the science of flying hot-air balloons and other aerostats, see *aerostat*.

bark: a small rowboat or sailboat.

dark lantern: a lantern with an opaque shutter which can be opened and closed to reveal and conceal the light inside it without extinguishing the flame.

dauphin: a French title for the eldest son of the king of France, and heir apparent.

fire lance: a long stick or spear with a firework attached to one end.

launch: a large boat carried by a ship.

livre: a French unit of currency, similar to the British pound.

louis: a gold coin minted in France.

mademoiselle: a French title for a female, either a young girl or an unmarried woman, similar to the English title "miss."

marquis: a French title for a male nobleman.

marquise: a French title for the wife of a marquis.

messieurs: the plural of "monsieur," see *monsieur*.

monsieur: a French title for a male, similar to the English title "mister."

necrology: a list of people who have died.

toise: a French unit of measure with a length of six feet.

urbanity: politeness of manner or courteousness.